Anguish

Novel

Anguish

Abdenal Carvalho

Copyright ® Abdenal Carvalho 2020

Title: Anguish

Category: Fiction Novel

Cover Designer: The author

Review / Layout: The author

Format: "6 x9" / 117 pages

Published Date: 07/2020

Author's translation

This is a work of fiction. Its purpose is to entertain people. Names, characters, places and events described are products of the author's imagination. Any resemblance to real names, dates and events are coincidental.

This work follows the rules of the New Spelling of the Portuguese Language. All rights reserved.

The storage and / or reproduction of any part of this work, by any means - tangible or intangible - without the written consent of the author, is prohibited. The violation of copyright is a crime established in law No. 9,610 / 98 and punished by article 184 of the Brazilian penal code.

SUMÁRIO

Chapter 1 - The Trunk 7

Chapter 2 - The Journey 29

Chapter 3 - The Persecution 49

Chapter 4 - Back to Captivity 69

Chapter 5 - The Invasion 87

Chapter 6 - The Freedom Prize 107

Chapter 1 - The Trunk

After four days chained to that tree after being cruelly whipped by orders from the farm foreman, she endured sun and rain determined to get out of there alive. That was the first time she was taken to be beaten in the trunk for running away from her master who habitually raped her.

Days before that stage, her attackers captured her and for several hours she was under the whip of the feared Baron of Café, as the one who bought it was known. Then they beat her with kicks and kicks, leaving her body full of serious wounds and bruises, she was bleeding a lot, blood was dripping from her mouth and nose.

Many others who lived there in the same situation saw the terrible way in which she found herself, but they could do nothing, since they were also deprived of the same freedom, the only thing to do was to see everything in silence. But, to better understand his sad story we need to go back in time, when it all started.

His name was Lucinete, whose meaning in the Afro-Brazilian dictionary, is: "One that is full of Light", affectionately called by those closest to him "Luz". She was born in a small Angolan village and came to Brazil when she was still small, the daughter of a slave couple who were bought by the Dantas, a very rich family and owner of many lands in the south of the country.

With coffee plantations, black pepper, sugar cane and several mills where they produced brandy on a large scale, mainly the best quality cachaça of the time. Upon arriving in Porto and disembarking from the slave ship, in 1822, more than thirty families were taken to one of its many farms and placed in accommodation, where they would live the rest of their lives, serving their masters.

There, they would have no rights and could not claim essential benefits for themselves or their children, such as a good school, quality food and various treatments that were given only to whites.

While the men worked hard in the cane fields, in exchange for a plate of food of the worst kind, their women and children served in every way possible in their owners' houses and were exploited there.

Luz, when she was ten years old, was raped by Mr. Albuquerque, son of Baron Dantas, of great reputation in those bands and whose malice against his slaves was notorious Abá, his father, whose name in Afro-Brazilian means "Hope", lost the court and decided to take justice into his own hands against the damn pedophile.

One morning, during his usual walk through the cane fields, garnished by some of his thugs, the unfortunate man passed by the part where the angry black man was in the company of dozens of other slaves working in the cane cutting, when he was attacked and his head was cut by a machete. .

The attack was by surprise and so fast that the pervert did not even notice the approach of death that riot awaited him, he did not have time for his protectors to prevent such violence. With the help of five other men, Abá killed the companions of that unfortunate man.

And they hid their bodies in shallow holes in the middle of the plantation. Days passed without being found, despite the great search made by the thugs and they were already considered dead. Baron Dantas then ordered that all the slaves who worked in the cane fields, coffee and black pepper plantations were to be gathered in a certain wing of his property and under heavy lashes they were forced to reveal what had actually happened to their son.

After hours under the heat of the whip, one of those who helped her father avenge his daughter's honor decided to give in and open his mouth, revealing what they had done. Ajagunã, despite his name meaning "Strong Warrior", chickened out in the face of the martyrdom he suffered and denounced everyone involved in the murder, denouncing Abá as the mentor of the barbarism committed against the little Albuquerque a few days ago amid the cane fields, where they worked.

After reporting in detail to his executioners how they committed the crime, the black snitch, who thought he would receive some benefit for having handed over his brothers, was beheaded. Abá and the others who helped him in revenge against the one who took the honor of his daughter as a child were taken to the presence of the Baron who had them executed in a perverse way.

The men were tied to a log and after being heavily beaten they perished in the flames. Everything happened before their families, who watched everything without being able to do anything to defend them, as they encountered armed thugs to the teeth, so they only mourned. Women, children and other family members remained terrified, mourning the death of their parents, spouses and relatives. They were cooked inside a huge fire that was raised around them still alive.

His cries of pain and despair at having his flesh consumed by the flames were terrible. And they could be heard in the distance. That horror scene would never be forgotten by those present, the infamous punishment was made so that the others would learn to fear their masters.

Indianara, Abá's wife and Luz's mother, was also killed. Her name means "The nearest native", she was the first and only woman to whom Abá gave her heart since adolescence. Their families were very close and early on they began to take an interest in each other.

With the invasion of the Portuguese in their country of origin in search of slaves, the dream of happiness that united that couple ended up becoming a cruel reality of pain and suffering, which resulted in that tragedy.

Soon after killing his son's murderers at the burning fire, Baron Dantas ordered his families to be executed and Indianara was one of those who lost his life. However, Luz remained alive because she was a child and because Joana, the youngest daughter of the fearful Baron became attached to her. By vehemently defending her before her angry father, claiming her innocence in the face of what had happened, he was able to save her.

Since then the little slave has lived in the mansion. After the death of his youngest heir, the old Baron went into depression and began to live in seclusion in his rooms, handing over the administration of all his goods to Dionísio Dantas, the eldest son. This one was worse than his father in malice, he treated slaves more harshly and there was no lack of severe punishment for those who, in his view, committed infractions worthy of punishment. He loved to see blacks in the trunk, taking lashes and laughing at his pains and he followed the same example as his younger brother in the practice of pedophilia.

He used to abuse girls, daughters of slaves. Without anyone daring to complain or try to stop him, because he threatened everyone with the burning fire as his evil father had done against those who sought to avenge his youngest brother's folly.

Luz's eyes were able to witness, in addition to the cruel death of his parents and those who helped him defend his honor, the suffering of countless other blacks who were taken to punishment in that accursed trunk. The years passed and the black girl who had been cowardly raped by one of the lords of the Dantas family grew up to be a beautiful and educated woman.

Despite the mediocre origin of slavery, it had a refined style, all due to the support received from its protector, Joana, daughter of the former Baron and sister of Dionísio, the current lord of those lands. But, despite all the protection she received, she was still a black woman with no freedom and any privilege as a human being. Aware of this, her master began to court her and wanted at all costs to possess her, however, the young woman refused to satisfy her wishes.

For that reason, one day he demanded that she go to his office to set up his library, which was composed of dozens of books. He was supposed to clean the place and put everything in order, which he did without hesitation, as he understood what his obligation was. It was on that occasion that he attacked her savagely for the first time and possessed her. Despite fighting a lot against the unexpected attack of the violent man, who seemed enraged and dominated by the desire to possess her, he was not strong enough to prevent the consummation of the act. After he had quenched his savagery, he still despised his victim. Mocking that which for a long time was the target of her filthy fantasies.

Dionísio expels her from there and orders that nothing of the event be reported to anyone, with the risk of being punished. He feared that his father would know of the infamous act committed against the one whom his sister protected. That would be bad for his image, they would lose his respect, for that reason keeping the false role of a sensible son was extremely necessary to receive the title of Baron From Coffee, belonging until then to his father.

Which would pass to him in a short time because he was very sick and threatened with death. Frightened by the threats made by the enemy, knowing that she was malicious and keeping his cruel promises, she decided to keep quiet, but the affliction remained on her face.

Alabá, whose name meant "Child Spirit", was the daughter of one of the black women who served the Dantas at the mansion. As his best friend and faithful confessor, he revealed to her all his secrets and kept nothing hidden about everything that happened to him, but even she did not have the courage to tell what she had suffered that day under the attack of that monster. However, she was unable to hide from her all the anguish that afflicted her soul, and began to be questioned:

— Come on, Luz, stop trying to deceive me and tell me what happened to you with that frown on your face

— Stop being curious, Alabá, there's nothing wrong with me

— If I didn't, I wouldn't be insisting that you tell me, come on, tell me what happened!

— Your curiosity is terrible, my friend!

— What's wrong with wanting to help a distressed friend?

— Your attitude is very generous and worthy of admiration, Alabá, but I have nothing to share with you right now. It is all a bad impression on your part that there is some problem, but my friend is wrong, everything is going well with me.

— Hum .. I know. If you think it convinces me otherwise, you are sadly mistaken. I know you very well, so don't waste your time with excuses!

— What a stubborn woman!

— I am, and you can be sure that I will find out what happened to you! Friend, I owe you a lot. If today I have a little education and I even know how to express myself correctly it was you who brought me up, I don't like to see you sad

— Well don't be worried about me, I'm fine

The dialogue between the two friends is interrupted by the arrival of Joana who orders Alabá to go and perform her chores in the kitchen in the company of the other maids, while Luz kept her company, reading a short story written by Machado de Assis, Brazilian writer, dated in the year. from 1884, whose title was "Chapter of the Hats" and which portrayed the hypocrisy, represented by the use of social masks, shown there in the form of hats.

The slave adopted by the youngest daughter of the Dantas received the best education available in the region at that time and one of her duties was to read to her godmother, which she did with great pleasure, as she was grateful for all the opportunities she received, including to be able to study and learn to read, which was prohibited for the children of slaves. However, at that time he would not be showing the same enthusiasm as before when reading, his words were empty, without the usual intonation.

ANGUISH – Novel

What led Joana to ask if something was happening to her

— Is there a problem, my daughter? I'm finding you so discouraged today

— No, ma'am, just a little indisposition

— You, unwilling to read good stories, since when?

— Yes, there is always a first time for everything in life, godmother. Today I find myself like this, without much courage

— Well, if you are still so discouraged I allow you to retire to your quarters to rest and tomorrow I hope you are already recovered to continue reading, because I am eager to hear about this story that seems to be very interesting

— It's ok. So, with your license ...

After leaving there, she was reclusive in the small room located at the back of the mansion, properly furnished with some furniture rejected by her ladies, due to the advanced time of use. In order not to be burned because it was a legacy of the family's ancient ancestors, Joana interceded with Dorotéia, her mother, to donate to the adopted slave's rooms to avoid waste.

The biggest problem in all of this was that there was no lock on the door to the room that guaranteed to prevent the unexpected entry of anyone intending to invade the place. There was only an old lock made of wood that with some effort it was possible to break and enter the enclosure and that night Luz went to bed earlier than usual, drunk with sleep for unhappiness and forgot to put the lock on the door.

Further increasing the little security of the place. It was dawn and everyone was asleep, when someone was walking slowly towards the small compartment.

Where the young woman slept. A lamp remained lit to illuminate the room and it was easy for the invader to access the interior of the room while the girl was lying on a bed, totally unprotected. The evil element leans the door again and latches on, after being sure that no one else would enter it, approached the victim who was in a deep sleep to the point of not hearing the noise of the invader's arrival.

But, when her mouth was muffled by one of the pervert's hands, she ended up waking up, however, prevented from screaming for help. Her aggressor was Dionysus, who for the second time possessed her. With his strong arms, he held her with such strength that he could not even kick or free himself from his sudden attacks.

Wearing only an appropriate dress for sleeping, without underwear, she facilitated the rapist's invasion of her sex. The woman squirmed on the bed as she could and cried out at the pain felt by each sudden move made by the pervert.

Minutes later, a hot liquid was poured into her vagina, the same filthy product that would continue the shame on her face the next day when she remembered that she had become a slut always forcibly possessed by her master at the time and place he wish. It even happened there, in his room, while he slept. After satisfying his selfish will he withdraws without showing any remorse.

He left behind a woman violated in her deepest intimacy, ashamed, feeling like the worst person in the world. The next morning she takes a long time to arrive at the mansion, where her lady was waiting for her to read the book with the story she longed to know. As he was surprised by his absence, he ordered Alabá to see the reason for the delay.

What was taken care of by strides. As soon as he entered the cramped place, he quickly realized that something bad had happened to his friend who was still lying on the bed in complete dismay. His terrible appearance denounced that he would not have had a good night's sleep, his clothes were torn and with some reddish stains, accusing some type of violence.

. — Luz, what happened? The godmother is pissed off with you because she didn't go to the big house to read the book!

Silence was the only response received in the face of the question, which made Alabá even more worried, shaking the young woman who remained motionless on the bed.

— Hey, wake up, woman! The godmother calls you! Has something happened to you? And that here incarnated in the sheet is blood?

After being disturbed for a long time, Luz turns to the annoying friend and gives him a harsh answer.

— For God's sake, leave me alone!

— How can I do that, you crazy, if the godmother calls you there at the big house? Get up soon and come, let's wait for you!

— I can't, tell her I'm not feeling well

— And since when can we make excuses for her, woman, are you crazy? Come on, stop talking and let's go at once!

Luz, sits on the mattress made of a thick cloth, filled with a type of granular material, generally used at that time and, looking steadily at her friend, explains:

— Please tell my godmother that I'm not well

And I won't be able to answer her call now, later I'll go over there and explain everything, okay?

— It's not good, Luz, if you know that you haven't answered your call to stay asleep, you can get irritated and send you to the trunk, see?

— Stop being stupid, girl, where the godmother would do that to someone. Come back and tell me I'm on my way!

— Nothing like that, I'll wait for you, she ordered me to just come back with you

— So wait...

— And these stains here on the sheet?

— Do you want to stop being curious, woman?

Alabá's insistence ended up encouraging Luz to go and see Joana, despite the fact that she was writhing in pain in her private parts and throughout her body, due to the sudden way in which her attacker had possessed her the night before.

Arriving in front of the one who out of respect used to call her godmother, she was unable to hide her discomfort, which was immediately noticed by her, even with her efforts to avoid it.

— Are you all right, my daughter? It looks so dejected, did something happen?

— Nothing too serious, godmother, is that lately I've been feeling a little sick

— And what could it be? I will send Martim to the city to call Dr. Rogério to come and observe him.

ANGUISH – Novel

Now please read the story I've waited too long and I look forward to hearing it

— Yes ma'am

That morning, the young woman who had been the victim of brutal rape a few hours ago once again tried to hide from her protector and those closest to her the pain and shame that burned inside her, so that her situation in the face of other residents of the place, as it would be terrible to be seen as some vagabond who was used by his master in order to satisfy his sexual whims.

The farm was a few kilometers from the city and Martim, a young slave who was a great admirer of young Luz and tirelessly tried to court her, but without success, went in a hurry to request the doctor to come and examine her. Joana's call for the doctor tormented the poor girl, as she knew that her secret could be revealed.

But, if she could count on the protection of her godmother who, since she was a child, freed her from the hands of her violent father and kept her safe for so many years, why she refused to ask for his help again, against the one who tormented her?

In those days, women did not have any form of rights and were treated inhumanly. His importance as a person was limited to serving his husbands and giving them children. In light of this, she knew that if the abuses suffered by Dionísio were made public, it would come to naught. And the result would be to be severely punished in the trunk for accusing his master. Besides that.

Even if he had how to prove the rape suffered by the farmer, it would be useless, since in the end it was his property, which allowed him to do whatever he wanted. Joana was a decent, honest and good-hearted woman, however.

She would have neither the strength nor the means to stop her brother's infamous actions against the slave. The only thing he could do in favor of the young woman was to keep her by his side and educate her, to propose a more peaceful life and away from the hard work in the slave quarters.

There it was hell for those who lived in slavery, a lot of pain and humiliation and tiredness. Many times she had the opportunity to witness the injustices committed against others with dark skin like her. It hurt him to see them suffering the terrible hardships in the cane fields and in the most arid parts of the different properties owned by their masters and he regretted not having the means to help them.

So what good would it do to reveal to her or to anyone her distress? Luz hated the men of the Dantas family, not only because they enslaved her to her people from her homeland, but because they murdered her parents in a monstrous and ruthless way before their innocent eyes, when she was still just a child , all because his father wanted to do justice against the unfortunate man who took his honor.

At the time Dionysus, the monster who currently abuses his body with impunity, was still very young. However, he witnessed the evils committed by his father with joy. He seemed to carry within him the same lack of character and compassion characteristic of that accursed family, with the exception, of course, of Joan who always protected her. The worst of all was having to live with the disgusting presence of the pervert who abused him inside that house, serving and respecting him as his master. Without being able to make any refusal and still with the risk of severe punishment. She felt bad, with constant nausea, she was old enough to understand what it was about, maybe she had become pregnant with the monster that raped her.

His physical appearance began to wither and it became impossible to hide the enormous secret that plagued his conscience. The next day Martim would arrive with the doctor who would assess his health and everything would be made public. There were only two ways to resolve that situation, revealing to Joana what had been happening or running away from everything and everyone.

That morning his choice was to disappear without a trace. So he got a small bundle of the most needed clothes and went out into the world during the night. The farm was very extensive and full of gunmen, but since she was a little girl she was smart to escape their attentive eyes.

Several times in his adolescence he left those lands and went to visit other places on horseback, even catching ear tugs from his godmother when he returned. All that damnation would now serve him to escape unnoticed from the astute watchmen who had the Baron's express order to shoot at anyone who moved.

The night was cold and the path was full of dangers, but his willingness to flee far from the damned man who raped her and the accusing looks that would certainly appear to disdain her shameful state made her go ahead.

She spent part of her life in the mansion, being treated well by Joana who had her as a daughter, received different treatment from other slaves, who would believe that the reason for her misfortune came precisely from the farmer who welcomed her into her home?

They would certainly say that she was pregnant with some black man, trying to blame her master for getting along in life. If others like her were not to think that way, but surely the other relatives and subordinates of the miserable would accuse her of that.

His thoughts seemed to be boiling as he walked through the woods towards the main road that was supposed to be about three miles away. Luckily that route was not strange to him, he knew like nobody else where he put his feet. How could he reveal to Mrs. that he was being abused by the unfortunate man? She was still a slave and despite everything belonged to her. How to demand reparation for the mistakes of those who even the wild animals feared, due to the immensity of their evil?

The end of everything was to go straight to the trunk, he knew that and for that reason he took the steps as far as possible from all that and what could happen to him in the worst case if everything were revealed. He did not understand the reasons that led the damn to have so much desire for her, after all, he was just a slave like all the others. Was it because he had a beautiful pair of legs and hips to envy many white girls?

It was Mr. Ambrósio who told him about these things, he was a strange man who lived a short distance from those lands, had yellow skin and was therefore not a slave. He was said to be the son of a Portuguese man full of money that he crossed with a certain Oriental, and that generated such a strange-looking man.

She lived in a huge house, there were several blacks there, however, none of them went to the trunk because of nonsense or lived thrown by moths, eating pig food and suffering the misery of the cane fields like those she knew on the farm where she grew up.

As I walked on my feet, time among bushes, time in the darkness of the dense forest, I reflected on these things. He was thinking of going again to the old man's house that he had met one of the times he had distanced himself from the Dantas' property, in one of his adventures on horseback.

Without Joana knowing it. He was the one who taught her the way back and was close to being lost in the forest that late afternoon. He seemed to be a person of good character, attentive and full of respect, perhaps if I told him about his drama, I could help him in some way. The dawn darkness finally started to fade, the sun came up on the horizon and the walk was made easier by the light. He could have sat under a tree, rested, but he preferred to continue his journey.

He grew up watching what happened to the slaves who dared to escape from the slave quarters, very early the sniffer dogs and their hunting dogs went out looking for the poor blacks and at the end of the day they returned with them dragged by the iron rings attached to their necks.

They stood in line, connected to each other, pulled like animals and beaten all the time by butchers who were paid to pluck their skins through the whip. Then they were taken to the log where they were picked up even more. If they did not die after the immense beating, they left there with their backs marked by the ferocity of the lashes that were shaken by the executioners. He knew that if he returned, he would lose all the good life he always received, due to the protection of Joana who welcomed her since her parents were killed.

Undoubtedly, Dionysus would use that act as an excuse to punish him. He would reverse what his sister did by denying her certain privileges and send her to punishment on the trunk or at least put her out of the Casa Grande, where she stayed with her godmother, and would be treated like any slave. Thus, without the care received from Joana, she would be at the mercy of the scoundrel to serve him as a sex slave as much as he wished. He could not return, he made the decision to flee that miserable situation.

And now he would rather die at the hands of the gunmen who came after him than return. With the arrival of the new morning and the path clearly looming ahead of him, the fugitive moves on without even thinking about stopping his hurried walk, as he was aware that by now the trackers were already on his trail. He would need to walk at least another two kilometers and reach the lands of the old friend in whom he would find shelter and protection.

At a certain point he decided to leave the branch where he practically ran and again he went into the forest, because he would undoubtedly be easy prey if he were exposed that way, because the gunmen would be circulating on all the roads in the place looking for him.

As a woman, they believed they would not be able to escape into the closed forest, full of harmful animals, but they were sadly mistaken because since they were children, they had been around and knew everything like the back of their hand.

It was already close to noon, the sun was high and hunger with tiredness dominated his body fatigued by the long journey. He was climbing a high hill when his almost faint eyes saw the roof of the house in the distance. It was planted in the middle of the forest, aged for many years, surrounded by the planting of several fruit trees. He had a stall with some horses and other creations, a huge chestnut tree so high that it gave the impression of its branches hitting the clouds, many servants took care of their chores because no one was called a slave there.

He accelerated his steps even more and in a few minutes he was facing the entrance door. Rosario, one of the servants, came to meet her and gave her a big hug, announcing her arrival.

Dona Benedita, a very thin and short woman, with eyes wide at the corners, with a wide smile on her lips came right up to meet the girl who was wearing a pink dress, with a blue belt and who seemed to have been torn in a fight against a wild tiger or something like that, asking scared about the reason for that alarming situation in which the maiden found herself.

— My God, but what happened to you, girl? Look at what condition this poor girl is in!

She was barely able to steady herself. Dirty, with her clothes in tatters, a leather sandal attached to her filthy feet with so much dirt, due to the long trail followed up there, her condition was critical and pitiful. His black skin was purple from exposure to the scorching midday sun, sweat was still running down his forehead and if he was slow to arrive at his destination, he might have fainted.

— Take her inside and prepare a bath so that this poor girl can cool off, then serve something to eat! Sebastião, quickly, go to the coffee plantation to call Ambrósio. Tell him that young Luz arrived here in a difficult situation and in need of our help. Come on, man, hurry up!

— Yes, I'll be going soon!

After being attended by women and well fed she rested. He stayed in one of the rooms of the house and remained there from the boring day. The old half-breed and his wife tried to understand what would have happened to the young woman so that she would suddenly appear on his property. It should have been something very serious to find yourself in that sad situation. They waited anxiously for her to wake up and put an end to so many questions. Ambrósio insisted that they should send a messenger to the Baron's farm.

In order to inform her of the girl's sudden arrival in their lands, perhaps he would then clarify the reasons for all this. However, Benedita, his wife, was more cautious and thought it best to wait for Luz to tell her own version of the facts before making any decision on the case.

For everything indicated that something very serious had happened to make her run away like that. The woman lived in that region for many years and knew the bad reputation of the Dantas, knew the despicable way in which they treated blacks and his exploitation cases towards their slaves, abusing them sexually without anything preventing him from such barbarity, making use of power that the law gave him as their lord and the title of Baron that was attributed to him, symbolizing power and autonomy over everything that was under his tutelage.

At that time the great landowners, coffee plantations, slaves and sugar cane mills were the Barons or Colonels who dominated everything and everyone who was in a lower social and economic position than theirs.

The greater the extent of their properties, the greater their dominance in the region. Nothing was exceedingly superior to them, they did not fear or respond to any form of justice other than their own, whatever their hands did right there was buried and forgotten.

Because of that, they did everything they wanted, without fearing any form of punishment. His orders were immediately carried out by his gunmen and a battalion of men who were always well armed to the teeth were on hand to carry out their determinations. While the fugitive rested in the care of the elderly couple, not far from there Dionysus confronted his sister, accusing her of covering for the slave's escape.

— You saw what resulted in the exaggerated protection that that damned slave gave, Joana, she ended up making her think she was free to leave these lands when she liked, since she was a girl she always had the habit of going over everything and everyone, always doing what it felt like on the tile!

— Luz has always been my responsibility, not yours, my brother. It was me and not you that Dad entrusted his care to, so let me take care of it myself, as I always did

— Negative, this time I will be the one to take the reins of this brave mule! Besides, Daddy is no longer in charge here and I make the decisions. From now on you will limit yourself to giving orders only to the house servants, in their chores. Luz becomes my responsibility, I will put a halter on the neck of that angry donkey!

— Don't you dare touch a single hair on my girl, Dionysus!

— I will not only touch your hair, but the whole body, when I find that damn runaway I will send her to the trunk!

— I swear to God, if you dare do her any harm I ...

Joana is silenced by Dionísio who holds her roughly by the arms and threatens her.

— What will you do, Joana? Will you stop me from giving that bitch the treatment she always deserved to get in that house?

The time of privilege is over for your protégé, sister, from now on she will be treated like any other black woman within my lands! Dionísio left there determined to start an intense search around the surroundings to find the slave who had escaped,

Giving orders to his gunmen to turn all other properties in the region upside down Until he found her and anyone who refused to cooperate with searches that were punished with the necessary rigor. A letter was sent by the Baron to the other slave traders in the provinces to cooperate and if they knew any information about the fugitive's whereabouts, to inform him urgently.

Orders received dozens of men spread from North to South, East to West of the region in search of clues that led to the whereabouts of the black woman who was hidden in the residence of Ambrósio and Benedita, now aware of all the events and decided to support and protect the poor girl from the clutches of the unfortunate.

— So, do you mean that demon has been abusing you all this time, my daughter?

— Yes, and now I decided not to subject myself to the whims of that monster

— Of course, my poor girl, did very well

— But you will have to pay a high price for your freedom, young lady

— I know that, Mr. Ambrósio, and that's why I don't intend to stay here with you

— And where would you go, my daughter? There is no one who can protect her in these parts, everyone is afraid of the demonized. Negative, you will be under our protection, that devil will not dare invade our home to take you from here

— Thank you very much for the gesture of goodwill to help me.

Dona Benedita, but you have no idea what that bastard is capable of, you will not only be able to invade your house to take me, but you will not hesitate to kill anyone who tries to stop you from fulfill your cruel intentions. I will not put you in danger because of me

— Luz is right, my dear, we have heard about all the barbarities that this man has committed in this region without any punishment, it is best to help her so that she can continue her escape safely.

— And what do you propose, Ambrose?

— Let us prepare two horses with supplies for a few days of travel, order one of our best servants to accompany her and give her the address of Justino, our son. He lives near Black gold, in the village of waterfall from Camp, surely this evil being will not find her there

— It is true, my girl, I had forgotten that. Our son is a wealthy merchant from that area, it will not be difficult to locate him

— I am very grateful for everything you are doing for me, I don't even know how I can ever thank you

— Thank us for staying alive and free from the clutches of that damn rapist

— I will do everything possible to make it happen, I promise After everything is ready and without wasting time the young woman.

And the guide, who was chosen by the elderly couple to take her to her new destination, continued on their journey, taking a path opposite to what would possibly be followed by the Dagestan thugs, on a long and unknown path until then for her.

Chapter 2 - The Journey

The municipality of waterfall from Camp,, where he was heading, was known for its very important gold reserves that existed in the 18th century, when the Portuguese exported around 800 tons of valuable ore to the Portuguese crown.

Most of the families that resided in that part of the country came from former miners and Justino was one of those who dared to go and live in that region where there was no longer a living from the extraction of the old ore. Despite the end of gold mining, the place was profitable in many other ways and became a major trader.

Meanwhile along the way on the long journey, Luz believed that she was forever distancing herself from her place of martyrdom and could already taste the true freedom in the blowing of the wind that licked her face while riding on that animal, whose neighing reminded her of the times of your adolescence. Time when he set up others like him and could walk through the dense vegetation of coffee plantations. However, when fate writes a story and chooses someone to be its main character, there is no escape. No matter how much you try to go your own way, you will end up stuck in the web that was woven by him.

Just like an insect or animal after falling into the clutches of a terrible predator, paralyzed by its poison or prey, without being able to achieve the deliverance it so longs for. It was already the end of that summer afternoon and the sun was beginning to go down in search of rest, when the crash of a shot from a cartouche was heard through the silence of the forest, previously broken only by the sound of the footprints of the animals during the ride. .

The fugitive wore a white dress that she got from Benedita, in which she splashed red tastes of blood and part of the brains that came out of her guide's head, blown up in front of her.

The echo of his terrifying scream rang through the field covered by a light layer of grass that covered the roots of the bushes that spread from one end to the other, the animal that was riding was also startled by the noise of the shot and galloped away. She was aware of being chased by the thugs sent by that despicable man from whom she tried to keep her distance, her former owner, who had certainly recommended his capture, but thought she was able to escape unscathed from the chase.

The peace of the countryside, which was previously broken by the blast of a bullet fired from the rifle of one of the criminals and burst the skull of the poor devil who had been tasked with taking it to one of the municipalities near Black gold, was now undone again , through the hoof of horses that with their horseshoes dug that hard land in a gallop from hell.

The fugitive and her animal tore the winds that blew in that part of the land, where fate seemed to have determined a tragic end under the mud of blood. He knew nothing about that region, far from the farm where he grew up. However, those who remained in pursuit did not back down.

Because they knew that no matter how much she insisted on running away, she would be forced to surrender sooner or later. So they thought because the path they took to escape was a large and unknown labyrinth. However, since she was a little girl she learned to gallop very well and knew how to ride a horse, in the midst of all that running she did not lose her balance or the reins of the animal, she conducted herself in an excellent way and left behind the five thugs who intended to capture her.

At the end of the open field, the path she was following became a pine forest, the girl lets go of her horse and leads him on, but she stays behind. Get into the woods and walk on foot in another direction, unknown and having no idea where you would take it.

The men chasing her went on after the animal that continued to run down the narrow path until they finally realized they had been tricked and the fugitive had stayed behind. However, the time it took for them to realize the error gave the slave a long journey and the distance between her and the criminals became favorable.

It was beginning to get dark and what he heard were only the orchestras of the many insects scattered under the green grass scattered on the floor, like a green carpet under the pines. Crickets in heaps sang her songs as if it were a big party and she was the bridesmaid, listening and receiving the homage.

Without being able to see clearly in that darkness that formed with the descent of the sun and the arrival of the night, he decided to sit near the trunk of a tree. I heard the sound of the music found only in the dense woods, the singing of the insects that praise the Creator. Indianara, his mother, when he was still alive told him about these things.

It taught him that the earth had been created by Olódùmàré, name given to God, the Creator of the Universe. According to his Yorùbá tribe, nature's song was for his worship. She told him that it was necessary to respect natural laws and when he was in the middle of it, it would not cause any harm.

Avoided destroying plants, not cutting down a tree or breaking even one of its smallest branches without being in dire need. He explained that all those responsible for the devastation of nature would one day be accountable to Olódùmàré and their souls would burn before him.

Luz knew everything about these things by heart and joked about it, as she had learned from her mother that she was a practitioner of the various African "religions". Among them, Candomblé, which has Banta origins, having as root the kimbdomb kiamdomb or quicongo ndombe, both meaning "black", have become synonymous and a generic reference of different expressions of religiosity of African origin.

If nothing that happened in the past had happened to your family, you would take over the mother's tasks. He would receive the mantle of Odum as an adult, serve the Orixá, and guide his people towards the worship of Olódùmàrè, whose meaning within the customs of his people is "Lord of destiny", "the beyond", "what we do not know, we know or imagine "," without limits ".

While reflecting on what he had learned from his mother, he allowed himself to rest his body ground by the truculent ride on Marino's loins at the foot of the tree with great branches. He was a remarkable animal and they had known each other for a long time, since when he was a girl he accidentally invaded the lands of Ambrósio, after getting lost during one of his antics. At that time he was still very young.

She was the one who put you in the first riding cell.

On that day he would take her to the home of the man who would possibly welcome her and, who knows, the ultimate freedom, but things ended up not being so easy. Due to the intense darkness it was impossible to have an idea of the time, whether it was still early in the evening or coming to an end. The orchestra of crickets continued to intonate several sounds produced by the mopping of their legs or wings, on each other, cicadas and hundreds of other animals praised Olódùmaré.

In the small pond nearby, some frogs and frogs also responded to insects with their weird songs and on top of the pine tree the owl participated in the big party with its strange and frightening humming. He settled down on the trunk where he chose to settle until dawn, and then went on, and there he took a nap. She woke up still in the dark under the singing of several birds that seemed to wake her up on purpose.

Without further waste of time, he got up from his rest and headed off, intending to get to the planned place. He did not know the exact direction or whether he would be going to the North, where Black gold was, or in reverse. She could not make the mistake of not realizing that she was going back to the house of the couple who helped her in the escape because the thugs would surely have passed by in search of her.

In those days, the clothes worn by women were huge and bulky, difficult to get around, but the black woman never liked to wear such exaggeration and dressed in dresses glued to her body despite the reprimand from her godmother. In this way it was possible to get around better and practice their crazy adventures.

How to ride a horse and go running through the lands of the Dantas, which were almost infinite. And, on that particular occasion, your clothes fit well. After all, they contributed greatly to enable him to run through the vegetation that at times was low, at other times high and dense, difficult to access.

Lost among so many thoughts, she hardly felt the immense tiredness that was gradually spreading through her body. He was still at large strides, when in the distance he saw a house surrounded by diverse plantations, the extensive yard and the yard surrounding various domestic animals made it clear that it was an inhabited place.

He approached cautiously and knocked on the front door in the hope of being received by someone who could help him. His expectations were right and a tall man, still young, with dark skin and an admirable physique appears almost naked, wearing only shorts, showing his strong muscles.

For the first time that woman who, since her childhood, experienced sex in a violent way and never felt any physical attraction for anyone, now found herself attracted to that stranger. Seeing him, his flesh shuddered inside. Embarrassed by what she felt at that moment without realizing that it would be impossible for the stranger to understand what was happening inside her, she looked down and raised her tired voice to ask for help.

— Please help me...

She said these words almost without a voice and the man held her tightly, when she was already collapsing from the intense tiredness, due to the long walk and for several hours without eating. After placing the visitor inside and settling her on a bed, despite the lack of comfort.

He wiped a damp cloth over her face in order to reduce the heat. He let her rest and meanwhile prepared something for her to eat when she woke up. The time Luz spent resting in the forest, where she could even get a few hours of sleep, could have been fatal if her pursuers had not lost their tracks. This was because when the fugitive left the mount, he went into the forest in the opposite direction from them, heading towards the East of the place where he was and they believed he had gone to the opposite direction.

While she was recovering from physical wear and tear the thugs returned to Ambrósio and Benedita's house, forcing them to tell where and how they could find her because they believed that she had found help there, as it actually happened. But the couple said they did not know their whereabouts for certain, but their excuses were not willingly accepted by the bandits who began to act more harshly.

As they were peaceful people and their servants had never dealt with such a situation, with many weapons they cowered and did not know how to react to free their masters who were badly treated by the invaders. After locking everyone in there in one of the many rooms in the house.

The men tied husband and wife to two chairs, opposite each other, forcing them to give them the information they wanted about the young woman under many threats and aggressions, both verbal and physical. Even after being victims of so many atrocities by the violent thugs, the couple limited themselves to nothing about the whereabouts of the young woman. Outraged by their insistence not to cooperate, they killed all the farmer's servants who were locked in one of the rooms of the house, they were murdered in cold blood by large-caliber shots. Benedita and Ambrósio said nothing because they knew that even if they spoke they would not escape certain death.

And they were not mistaken in this regard. The order given by Dionísio Dantas was that they use all the necessary means to obtain the results that would lead them to capture the fugitive and not leave witnesses. After being beaten with excessive cruelty, the couple was soaked in kerosene and set on fire, they were burned alive.

The large house surrounded by several fruit trees and whose land was extensive, with many creations of domestic animals, was the scene of that immense tragedy that befell the lives of good people and who had never practiced any form of evil before anyone. Then she was also set on fire and all of her expensive furniture incinerated. The high flames soon spread around the place, turning everything that was there to dust and ashes, including the bodies of the former inhabitants of the place.

Others who were working at the coffee plantations at that moment saw the long cloud of black smoke rising in the direction of the mansion and ran to see what it was all about. Great was the desperation of everyone when they arrived. Perplexed they wept and lamented when they realized that their masters' house was on fire and because there was no one outside the place, they immediately concluded that everyone had been killed together in the fire.

Even if at first they didn't understand how it came to be. In that region, there was no authority that could investigate what had happened, everything was resolved by the landowners, usually slaves. Some blacks escaped with their lives for not being present at the place. At the time of the carnage, they worked on the plantations and when they got there, they didn't know what to do, until someone had the idea of sending one of them looking for Justin. The son of the murdered couple, to let you know about recent events. That done, they looked for a way to take shelter.

Going to an old shack located among the coffee plantations until the new landlord arrived. In the meantime, Luz awakened and his new protector served him a broth made from various vegetables and free range chicken, he intended to give his strange visitor the necessary energy to explain his unexpected arrival, which she did as soon as she recovered.

— First I apologize for invading your property, but it was necessary

— Okay, no need to worry. Pleasure, my name is Florencio - I said that while kissing her hand - I see that you are quite cultured, despite your dark skin

— The pleasure is mine. I'm Lucinete, but they call me Luz, I was adopted by my lord's sister and educated by her as if she were her daughter

— I understand

— But I realize that you are a man as cultured as I am, did you also have someone who educated you?

— No, my education was acquired through my own efforts

— Yes, now I realize how many books you have here on this table

— Many of them belonged to my father who became a black man free from slavery when he received the freedom given by his master. This happened a few days before his death and he lived on this small piece of land that he inherited

— Lucky man, your father, after being released did you still receive a piece of land to live on?

— Yes, it seems strange, but that's exactly what happened.

He was highly esteemed by his owner and was bestowed in this way. Then he married my mother, another free slave, with whom he gave my life.

— So, as I understand it, your father's master freed several slaves

— There were only five

— And where are they all?

— They left, I'm not sure where they might be, but now enough about me, let's talk about you. How did you get here? After all this property far from the others and few would know how to find it

— To be honest I got here by chance, it was not my intention

— Got lost? And your animal, where is it?

— I abandoned him on the road, at the time I intended to go to the municipality by the name Field Waterfall, do you happen to know where it is?

— Yes, I know it very well, but if you intend to get to such a place because, then, you dispatched your animal? Has the horse become ill, suffered any serious injury or is it dead?

— None of that, when I dispatched it was quite salable

— I do not understand...

— It's ok. I am a fugitive and because I have some thugs on my trail I had to get rid of my animal to run away from them, going into the forest in order to lose them

— I understand. So that's how you ended up getting here?

— Exactly

— But you said you were a free slave, raised and educated by your former master's sister. How did you become a fugitive, commit a wrongdoing?

— No, I just got tired of being raped almost daily by that damn

— Who do you mean, actually?

— I grew up on the Dantas' property after witnessing the death of my parents, murdered by the former coffee Baron. At that time, as a child, I was forced to watch them burn alive in a fire right before my eyes

— My goodness, what a barbarity! And why did they do it, what mistake did they make to deserve such a terrible end?

— Since when do these slave demons need reasons to practice their crimes against unfortunate poor people like us blacks? Just for having dark skin we are targets of its aggressions and treated like garbage

— And did this happen as soon as they arrived in Brazil or after they were already established in the lands of the Barons?

— After being on his farm for a while. Our lord's youngest son raped me when I was just ten years old and my father couldn't stand what he did, so he joined with others and killed him in the cane fields. But, under a lot of pressure, one of them ended up revealing the secret and they ended up all dead, including my parents, who were consumed by the fire right in front of me without being able to save them.

— Miserable! This makes me indignant and further increases my desire to fight for the freedom of our people

— I share this desire.

But what else could we do against a multitude of enemies well armed and protected by the empire?

— Sometimes I stop to reflect that we are many blacks in this country. So why don't we unite and fight these oppressors and break free from this terrible yoke? What happens is that we are very passive, accommodated and cowardly!

— But we have no weapons and, even if we did, no slave would know how to use them

— Everything is learned, my friend, until you squeeze your finger on a trigger and send these damned Portuguese to hell!

— So you are in favor of a revolution?

— Yes, completely! But go on, tell me the rest of your story

— After the Baron fell ill and became unable to manage his assets, his son Dionísio, who for a long time already worked in the domain of properties and took decisions in his father's place, completely took control of everything, starting to govern even more severely. It was then that because he found himself with all the power he started to rape me whenever I was alone, away from the other people who lived in the mansion. Tired of so much abuse I decided to run away and now he sent his thugs after me to take me back.

— White wretch! A thousand times miserable! And why didn't you reveal everything to your protector, the one who raised and educated you?

— Think carefully: What could a poor woman without any power of authority, in a country where only men rule and govern, do to defend me?

— You're right, the poor thing would still put her life at risk

— Of course yes!

That worm wouldn't have the slightest remorse to kill her if she tried to come out in my defense.

— You did well to keep secret and run away from that monster.

— Don't worry, here with me you will be safe, nobody will harm you

— I appreciate your generosity, but we both know that I will never be safe while being chased by those wretched thugs

— Stay calm, this place is far away and it will not be easy for them to find you

— Don't be as if you don't understand the situation, Florencio, we know that if I got here they will also come

— Okay, I'm not going to stay here pretending I don't understand the danger we're in, so let's do it like this: I'll accompany you to your destination until you personally hand it over to the care of your friends' son, whom you should meet at first

— Very well, that is the right thing to do, because there he has influence and can keep me safe, if we stay here and my pursuers locate this place you will be killed. In addition to that I will be taken back to suffer the martyrdom of the punishment reserved for runaway slaves, in the hands of that diabolical man When she tries to get up she feels very dizzy and almost goes to the floor, but she is supported by Florencio's strong arms that do not let her fall.

— Let's take it easy! Miss is still not fully restored, rest some more

— It's ok

A strong sleep fell over his tired body and with it came the dreams that used to disturb his suffering soul.

He was able to review the arrival of blacks in the port, after traveling for several weeks on that filthy slave ship. Under the tyranny of the sea captains who were wicked Portuguese who whipped anyone who breathed too hard. It was like she was in that hell again, reliving that miserable life in its entirety.

All remained chained by their ankles and necks, linked to each other in a row, regardless of whether they were large or small. There were no differences, they were all black, they were nothing more than unfortunate slaves and they should be treated like scum of humanity.

It was the first time that he had left the African lands where he was born, one day he dreamed of leaving that region cursed by God, where his people never seemed to progress, despite their tribe living in peace. But not for a moment did he think it would be that way, dragged like raw animals and taken to another part of the world, where they would be made slaves and tortured on a log until death without their lives having any value.

As he slept and relived his past through the nightmare in which he found himself, his body shuddered. Florencio sat beside him the whole time while he slept and noticed his torment.

After arriving in Brazilian lands, they were all handed over to their masters who were already waiting for them, there they were sold for some coins as if they were miserable animals, irrational and who did not understand the suffering. Then they would be used in sugar cane plantations and coffee plantations. The mistreatment suffered there was indescribable, it hurt him immensely to remember the suffering of his people in the slave quarters and all the humiliations they were subjected to while she, helpless, could do nothing to help them. That dream, which seemed more like a deep torment, still made him relive the death of his parents at that fire.

Where mercilessly the flames consumed them alive. He seemed to be able to hear their screams clearly, all their despair, to feel the pain they felt as the flames ripped through their living flesh. She woke up in awe, her eyes were wide and a strong astonishment revealed the terror her soul had just witnessed.

— Calm down, it was just a dream!

— They're burning, I hear your screams!

— Calm down, who's burning?

— My parents, at the stake, are still alive, we need to save them!

He now understood his anguish, that nightmare brought back the bitter memories of the day his parents had been killed. Thrown alive into a fire by the damned Portuguese. He understood his pain, he could imagine how intense his suffering was.

Luz's awakening occurred just during the day's sleep and the rest of that night she was unable to go back to sleep, as she was very frightened by the mirages seen in the nightmare she had hours before. As soon as it was morning, the two arranged what was necessary for the long journey they would take.

Meanwhile, far away, Joana suffered without hearing from the one she learned to love as if she were her daughter. Every day her knees grated before the image of Our Lady of Mercy, begging him to protect her from all evil and keep her safe.

Alabá, his faithful friend kept mentioning his name to the other women who served there, died of longing and feared that something bad had happened to him.

Dionysus remained sour as usual, discounting the frustration of having lost the black woman with whom he satisfied his sexual desires. She was angry and demanded more efforts on the part of the thugs to find her as soon as possible.

Once, indignant at only hearing that the fugitive had simply disappeared and not even the most skilled scouts could locate her, he exploded in anger and ordered that the men whose mission to find her was unsuccessful were placed on the trunk and personally whipped them by dumping them on. his loins the hate that burned in his chest. The Baron's ferocity was so great that he started to run into his house, too, and hit his family. Mother and sister became the target of such a revolt and began to be threatened.

— That black bastard managed to escape right under my nose as if by charm! Not even the best of my men can find their tracks, and do you know whose fault this is all? The ladies! That's right, it was you two who spoiled that ordinary girl too much and made her think she was one of us, with the same rights to freedom that we have

— My son, she is a good girl. Understand that if Luz ran away from the farm it is because she must have her reasons, something must have happened to her

— Shut up, you useless old woman! Don't give me this absurd litany that that miserable woman deserves to be treated with the least dignity, she is no different from the other filthy blacks who serve this house and as soon as she is found she will pay dearly for the insolence with which she dared to challenge me

— Brother, see how you speak, respect our mother!

He hits the woman in the face with a strong blow that if it had not been delivered with an open hand she would have broken her jaw. Due to the violent attack the woman ended up falling on some of the furniture in the large room, being helped by the servants, after the odious man left.

That act of violence left Joana in bed for several days, her fragile body was badly bruised and her face became very purple. Martim, the black man who felt a strong passion for Luz, was a boy of only twenty-two years, very discreet and knew how to obey. He had little talk, he was never taken to the trunk for making unnecessary mistakes and he was very hardworking, which earned him praise from the overseers to the Baron. That afternoon he was summoned to appear before Dionysus

— Did my lord send for me?

— Yes, my boy, I am in urgent need of your services

— No, I'm here at your service

— I need you to go looking for that runaway slave and bring her back as soon as possible. I can no longer wait for these incompetents who only return empty-handed. I want you to choose the best horse in the stall, prepare it with the best mounts, feed it well and make sure you have everything you need for the trip with you. Then go to the four corners of these lands of my God and do not return until you find it and can bring it back to me. Did you understand what your mission is, boy?

— Yes sir, I will do as you ordered me

— So stop wasting time, go and follow the orders you received!

— Yes sir!

The obedient slave who had won the admiration of his masters from an early age for appearing to be more fearless than the other blacks, left there determined to carry out the orders received, even because it was not his custom to disobey.

Since childhood he was Luz's best friend and had a great appreciation for her. Her heart fell in love with the slave she would have to hunt and bring back. He knew that she would suffer in the trunk, however, the commitment to her master could not be undone because of the feelings that burned in her chest, she would follow reason and let her emotions fall into oblivion, she would return with the fugitive trapped in chains and hand it over to the Baron.

He would certainly be highly praised for his achievement, would become his trusted man who would place him among the foremen of his many lands and would give pride to his family, as well as his people. In contrast to this, if he disobeyed the ordinances that were imposed on him, he would end up as Luz on one of several trunks under painful lashes.

Unlimited shame would pour over the name of his parents, who as slaves had no value, but would start to be recognized among other blacks as privileged for having as their son a man who lived close to Baron from Coffee, and because of him honored.

Certainly that was a stupid pretense on the part of a young man who was still mistaken with futile pretensions, after all, when would a white and arrogant Portuguese like Dionísio bother to recognize the value of a black man? He was seen by him only as someone who was part of his property and had a duty to carry out his orders without owing him any favor. His prospects were immature and without foundation. However, his ambition went beyond the passion he felt for the woman he wanted from his youngest age.

Since they were born in the same African village and arrived together in Brazil. They were bought and taken to the same slave quarters where they became slaves, but apparently there was a mixed, impure feeling inside their chest, where love and envy burned.

He was not content to see that Luz had been more privileged, enjoying the support of Mrs. Joana, while he and his family, as well as the rest of the blacks, remained serving in the most arduous part of that land she lived in the comfort of the big house as if it was a white one. In his view, this unfair condition was an affront that could not be accepted, after all, Luz was as black and a slave as they were.

Because of this, the boy insisted on trying to attract his master's attention on himself, trying to win the same position among whites. He understood that if he fulfilled the mission that was given to him, bringing the fugitive back, he would show competence to be placed among the other thugs or, who knows, to assume the position of foreman on the farm.

This would already be a big step to change his current situation, raising him to a position above a simple slave. Therefore, he would not allow that great opportunity to be taken away from him.

He would pursue and find the fugitive, hand her over to Dionysus and receive the deserved respect. Would his thoughts really be right as to what fate had in store for him? Would Martim find the slave formerly endowed with greater privileges than he would, and would he receive from his master what he considered to be deserved for his great deed. Often unrestrained ambition leads us to make the mistake of believing in vain promises that are made to us, without first analyzing to see from whom they were promised. Men like Dionísio do not keep promises made to people he considers insignificant.

And for him Martim was nothing more than a wild animal to whom he had extreme powers to dominate, use the strength of his arm in favor of his own needs. In his view, that slave deserved nothing in return for his services, as he would only be doing his duty, any claim reserved the right to place him in the trunk. This was the truth of the facts, however, the ambitious young man was blinded by the intention of destroying the reputation of the girl he went on a hunt for, so that one day he could see her fallen under the punishment that awaited her.

In the meantime, he would be standing next to his master and the other foremen, watching the executioner delivering several blows to his meat from the ropes of the merciless whip. He would be happy to see her scream like any other black woman.

As he galloped at full speed down the dirt road that cut through the Dantas' lands, his eyes shone as if they were torches of fire, at last his ambition was externalized and his true traitor personality was revealed, if Luz could see him at that moment, maybe not would believe.

The black man of admirable physique, excellent knight, of good aim and without any qualms, went on a journey determined not to return without his prey. Luz was in danger, the order given was very clear: The fugitive should be brought back to its former owner, at any request, at any cost. And that would be done to the letter, he was determined to show good service.

Chapter 3 - The Persecution

At the same moment when the fugitive's new pursuer left in pursuit, in the small and distant property where she was protected by her new friend, danger is approaching, when ten of the men sent to find her find the hiding place and, even without knowing the sure if she was there, they decide to investigate. The one who seemed to be the leader of the gang approaches the house and seeks the presence of the resident.

— Oh, home, good morning!

The couple is frightened by the arrival of the thugs and Florencio immediately asks Luz to hide, then goes to meet them.

— Good morning, how can I help you?

— Good Morning. We are doing a search for the region in search of a slave who fled the lands of Baron from Coffee, Mr. Dionísio Dantas. We wonder if the friend in a certain way could not pass on some information that would help in the capture of the fugitive?

— I'm sorry, but so far I haven't seen anyone passing by these past few days, you are the first to pass in this direction

— That's right! Sorry for the inconvenience, we will continue on our way.

— I'm sorry I can't provide any help

— No problem, but surely others may come in that direction, as many men were assigned to go on this search for the missing slave. If you know of anything new, don't hesitate to collaborate, because denying the Baron any information is dangerous!

— I understand, I will certainly do that, I do not want enmity with my neighbors

Having dispatched the thugs, he returns to the interior of the house and warns of the danger they will be in if they remain there, however, to run away would be risky at that moment, since he could not be sure where they would be on the prowl.

— But they are already gone, shouldn't we enjoy it and get out of here before they decide to return?

— No, because I believe they doubted my answers. Surely they will be around here to see if I spoke the truth or if I tried to deceive them

— Miserable!

— They just didn't break into the house to make sure my words were true so as not to show that they doubted. They allow us to try to escape, so they would catch us with enormous ease

— You are absolutely right, we will stay here without them noticing my presence until they give up and leave

— Yes, we will do it that way

Justino was the only heir to Ambrósio and Benedita, the same couple who.

For not agreeing to pass on information about where the fugitive who dared to escape the clutches of the powerful Baron from Coffee, ended up being beaten and burned alive in his own home by the men of Dionysus.

After being notified by his parents' servants who escaped the attack unscathed, he returned accompanied by at least fifty men to the old region where he was born and from where he had left about ten years ago to become a successful man in the lands of gold. There he prospered and was successful in his purposes, became a great merchant and received the title of Count, married Gabriela, an important countess, from a wealthy family.

His return was in search of unveiling the cause of his parents' death and punishing the guilty and the fifty men who followed him to the property of Ambrose, his murdered father. They were all military personnel provided as their private garrison by the emperor.

Upon arriving there, he was received by the blacks who let him know about the situation. Aware of the cowardly way in which his parents were attacked and killed, he separated the garrison into four groups and sent them east, west, north and south in search of criminals.

The order given was that they arrest and take to their presence any and all suspects found in those lands, as long as they mounted a horse and were armed, they could use force and even retaliate against possible attacks by those who refused to surrender.

The scenario was one of the worst, on the one hand several thugs in pursuit of the fugitive from the power of the Dantas and on the other dozens of soldiers spread across the four corners of the region in an attempt to capture those responsible for the death of the elderly couple.

Without forgetting Luz, the young woman who, for not enduring the life of abuse suffered at the hands of her master, decided to flee from suffering. For two days she remained hidden in Florêncio's house, who occasionally went out on the ground to perform some tasks, such as weeding the place or planting some seeds in the spacious backyard, just to mislead her observers, giving them the impression of really find yourself alone on the property if you were even being watched.

At the end of the planned time, he prepared the mount and pretended to leave in the direction of the nearest city in order to be followed or that the bandits would try to enter the house to make sure that the slave was not really hiding in the place, that way they would leave the stakeout and the doubt about their permanence in the vicinity would end.

The boy was smart and took a large-caliber gun with plenty of ammunition. He pretended to gallop, but returned by another detour and positioned himself close to the property in order to be able to make some shots if the girl's pursuers dared to appear suddenly to invade her home. After a few hours the expected happened, the thugs appeared in number of four and positioned themselves in front of the doors.

In this, it became impossible to fight them at the same time. However, he thought that if the two who were in the yard were hit, the others would invade from the back and it would be inevitable to prevent the capture of the girl without putting her at risk. But what he did not know is that Luz was not the type to surrender without a fight and when he saw the siege he armed himself with a shotgun he found in the hideout, sending bullets at the invaders. When he realized what had happened, Florêncio fired almost simultaneously at the thugs in his sights.

One of those in the back was hit by shots fired by Luz, while the two positioned at the front were killed by shots from the owner of the house and a fourth member ran out into the woods, chased by the sniper who wanted to finish the job.

However, there were several fatal traps scattered throughout the forest, set in order to catch animals from beasts that could threaten their animals or hunts with which they fed. Unfortunately, the V was taken by surprise by one of them, falling into a deep pit where there were huge sticks in the shape of spears and he was smashed in four of them.

His cry of pain that spread through the forest indicated that his escape had come to an end, now he was to return to see how the girl was doing. Only after what happened did he realize that when chasing the enemy he left Luz alone and in danger, feeling the need to apologize.

— Sorry to have left you alone and went in pursuit of that thugs, is that I did not want him to escape

— No need to apologize, in your place you would have done the same

— Only the four remained in the stake, waiting for you to appear outside or for me to leave and they could invade, they knew that I lied when I said that I had not seen you

— Thankfully they didn't all remain, we wouldn't be able to handle

— But for sure they will be back soon, they must have just gone to scan the surroundings and if they heard the shots they are already galloping

— Certainly yes, we will take care of it before they arrive

The two quickly prepared the animals and left, leaving everything behind. The house, the few furniture, creations, plantations ... The property that Florêncio had received as an inheritance from his father and cultivated for a long time would be completely abandoned, at least for a while. The extensions of his lands were suitable for planting coffee, sugar cane or cattle for the vast pasture that existed there, although he never made use of such things.

In a forest like that, without the natural noise of urban centers and where only silence prevails, it is easy to hear the sound of a gunshot, especially if it was carried out by a large caliber weapon such as that used by the sniper. And as was expected, the other six men who had gone to find out the whereabouts of the slave in the immediate vicinity heard the shots and hurriedly returned, but luckily when they arrived they had already dispersed from the place.

Then they split into two groups and went after the fugitives, because they now knew that the black woman was under the protection of the man from whom they asked for information and were deceived. The couple was already miles away. They increasingly approached Field, Waterfall, where they intended to meet Justino, Ambrósio's son. What they did not know was that he had already come in that direction and would no longer be there, but on the old property where his parents were killed, in search of finding the culprits.

But, according to the plans designated by the destination, they would still have to confront a new threat before reaching the destination, as the worst was yet to come to both. It seemed that Lucinete had been born on a night of full moon or complete darkness.

And the name given to him did not match his lack of luck at that moment. Everything went wrong in the life of that poor woman who, since she was a child, suffered miserably.

While walking along the same path where days ago she was surrounded by the daggers of Dionysus and saw her guide with her head blown right in front of her, she cursed in thought the evil destiny that had always haunted her and that never allowed her to be happy.

In fact, I was scared of the possibility that the same scene would happen again and this time be the new friend to lose his life. They remained silent during the trip. A small space separated the two animals on which they mounted.

The silence was broken only by the pounding of the thick horseshoes caught in the horses' hooves, stepping on the gravel ground and accompanied by the blowing of the wind that insistently whistled in their ears.

Florencio kept an eye on everything that moved around, both below and flying across the sky, to avoid surprises. However, not even their whole experience was enough to not be surprised by the unexpected, as had happened on the previous occasion.

It turns out that this time there were not many enemies, it was just one and much more determined to take the fugitive to its owner than the previous ones. Luz was amazed to realize that the man with a rifle in his hands, pointing in the direction of her and her companion, was Martim. Someone he knew since he was a child and always considered him as a brother, whom he thought he could fully trust. Without clearly understanding his attitude, he asked:

— Martim, why is that?

— Do not ask me for anything, woman, you are a runaway slave and come with me. And if this guy wants to, he'll take lead

— I thought you were my friend, I saw you as a brother

— But I always wanted you as a woman and I was rejected all the time. Now it doesn't matter anymore, I will take you to the little sack and he will reward me, I will become a hired gun or farm foreman

— I do not believe you are trusting the promises of that monster, Martim, he will not fulfill anything he promised you

— Yes, he is a man of his word! And don't argue with me, go back in front of me, because I want to arrive at the farm until dawn

After disarming Florêncio, Martim leads them back to the Dantas farm along the main road without worrying about finding other thugs along the way, as he was under the protection of the most powerful man in those parts and if anyone dared to touch him he would be punished by the whip. Well, at least that was what he believed, but he forgot that the others had not been informed of his mission. thugs, gunmen, bounty hunters and all kinds of people were summoned by the slave.

They were hired on a mission to locate and take the black woman back, that region was filled with ambitious people who longed to be rewarded for doing so, finding them would be dangerous. They walked less than two kilometers in the opposite direction from where the couple had previously gone, when the echo of a gunshot was heard and the buzz of a bullet scraped the ears of the black man who was driving the two prisoners, forcing him to a sudden maneuver to avoid be killed. In a shout he ordered the couple to go behind some huge rocks located in the open field.

To protect themselves. The three of them being there, the exchange of gunfire between Martim and the men who sought to take possession of the fugitive began, there were two in number who sought to take her life. Florencio insisted that he be allowed to use his rifle to help in defense, but the black man was stubborn and ordered him not to dare to touch the weapon. After many shots he ran out of bullets.

The opponents realized the situation and left the place of defense, shooting continuously at the rocks that protected the three in the intention of approaching and dominating them, but Florêncio was skilled in handling the rifle and quickly solved the problem. With his weapon, even without the consent of the gunman who was driving him, he shot at the two opponents who fell face down. That done, he turns and points to Martim with the two pipes still smoking.

With the finger attached to the trigger, it was enough to breathe harder or to move sharply and a shot would be fired. Luz, who until then remained lying on the ground to protect herself from the bludgers that swirled through the walls made of stones, jumps up and places herself between the two enemies.

Ordering them to end the threat. She was a friend of the two men and did not want the death of either of them.

— Stop it! Put those weapons down, for the love of God, no more deaths!

— Tell him to download it first, then I'll drop it too!

— You heard, Florencio, answer!

— Don't be childish, Luz, this bastard has no interest in keeping me alive, if I do what he asks he'll blow my brains out!

— Okay, so the two will do it together, at the same time. Or, if you really want to kill yourself, you can shoot through me!

The two men, whose eyes were more fierce than a wild tiger, soften at the words of the woman who deep down learned to love and disarmed herself. Luz picks up the two rifles and leaves on horseback, in a strong gallop. Because of the attack suffered during the journey, he decides to take a shortcut inside the forest to avoid further surprises. A

t dusk they stop at a certain point and decide to rest there. Luz, astutely, initiates a dialogue with her former friend in the hope of convincing him to give up giving her to the Baron from coffee, revealing to Martim the real reason for having fled the farm.

When he became aware that Dionisio had raped her and forced her to have sex with him whenever he wanted, he was indignant. The time it took between his escape and that moment was less than thirty days, it was still not possible to notice the pregnancy that until then he chose to hide even from Florêncio. Now was an ideal time to talk about it.

— I can't believe that all this time you hid it from me, was that the reason you got sick as soon as we met? I could have taken better care of you, the food ...

— Yes, Florencio, I have tried hard not to notice, I did not want to put more responsibility on your shoulders, because what you have done for me has been more than enough.

— And why didn't you tell Mrs. about what that devil from hell did?

— Martim, I am only a black woman, a slave like you and the others of our tribe.

Mrs. Joana loves me as if she were her daughter, but she has no power to get rid of the hands of that unfortunate

— Because if I already knew that I would have done justice with my own hands against that son of a mare, because I had a lot of chance!

— And at that time he would be in the trunk being flogged to death, that's not how we're going to solve things

— And what do you understand about slave life? He is black with smooth skin, I know your type, I never knew what it was like to work in the fields or in a cane field. He is well literate black, he speaks handsome

— That's right, I'm a free black, I'm not owned by anyone

— Soon I saw, you don't know about the fight that we slaves have to go through to survive in that hell

— It is not necessary to suffer the same injustices to understand a situation, even though I am free I understand the horror of slavery

— Can the two of you stop this rant and worry about a way for us to stay alive?

Despite the friendly conversation between the two men, Martim remained holding his gun. He was not less than four meters away, he seemed to fear that Luz was just trying to distract his attention so that he could be dominated and they could escape, so he took over the guard post while they rested for the long trip they would take the next morning. The silence of dawn was broken by the grunt of the owl, the party of insects and the light blowing of the wind that played with the vegetation, the watchman in the face of such calm believed that no threat was approaching.

And decided to lean against one of the many trees that existed there, under which they took shelter. Put your gun aside and light a cigarette. He exchanged his shrewd attention for a minute of distraction, wanted to taste the smoke that burned. But death was slowly approaching from there, treading softly on the dry leaves so as not to make a noise or awaken its victims.

The sound of a rifle shot echoed through the woods and the silence was interrupted once again by the accurate shot along with the thud of a heavy body on the ground. His fall was felt at the foot of the thick pequi tree, where the two blacks slept in a deep sleep. The smoke from the cigarette that burned in Martim's mouth was stained red after the blood spattered from his skull, burst by the bullet that came from the darkness.

Florêncio and Luz woke up frightened by the noise and didn't even have time to understand what had happened, they were already being dominated, arrested and tied up by the several men who arrived there in the dead of night without being noticed and waited for the best moment to attack. The girl looked at the body of her childhood friend with her eyes full of tears, as she was dragged along with her new companion of suffering.

The sun was rising behind the hill, when they were already led by the thugs to the Baron farm, where they would certainly be punished for the rebellion. She would receive the trunk as punishment, dozens of lashes applied by the hands of Dionysus himself and his escape partner could suffer the same punishments or be killed in the most horrendous way. Joana was the youngest daughter of the former Baron of Café and the younger sister of the cruel slave-maker, the same one who waited anxiously for the capture of the fugitive in order to punish her for daring to challenge her power.

His prayers were raised to heaven every day and at different times, interceding to the most powerful saints to protect his girl from her brother's cruelty. She still could not understand the reasons that led Luz to flee, and wondered if she had somehow been too strict with her.

— My daughter, don't be so upset about it, in no way was this slave's escape caused by anything related to you

— So show me another reason why my girl is so distressed that she decides to run away from this house, Mom?

— I don't know, Joana, but you were always so helpful in dealing with her that I can only understand that it was for another reason and not because of you

— I get distressed just thinking about what will happen to the poor thing after my brother puts his hands on her

— Well, about that we can already imagine what will happen

— It is true, at least it will be punished in the trunk, as he usually does with the other slaves

The conversation of the two women is ended and they go back to their duties, mother and daughter met in the yard of the big house, knitting. Since the flight of Luz, Joana has never again devoted herself to reading poetry books and romances with her passionate stories. She missed hearing her protégé's voice, reading beautiful tales of love that made her days happy.

Justin, wanting to take revenge for the cruel death suffered by his parents and some of his servants at the hands of the thugs, was determined to find out who was responsible for the massacre.

Therefore, after dividing their officers into groups, they went looking for clues that would lead them to clarify the case. It did not take long to learn from the comments made by people in nearby villages about the recent events, where the Baron of Café had ordered his men to go in search of the runaway slave to use whatever means necessary to locate his whereabouts and take her back to her property.

With this information in mind, he understood that this would have something to do with what happened to his parents and chose to go deeper in his investigations. Accompanied by three of the soldiers who arrived with him in the region, he immediately went to the Dantas' lands to obtain further clarification.

And when he got there he asked him to speak directly with the slave, which he was duly granted. Dionysus was a man of exaggerated stature, was almost two meters tall and weighed a little less than a hundred kilos. Light skin, typical of a good Portuguese, yellow eyes and a denture in the mouth full of gold.

His voice was soft, but at the same time malicious, his gaze was deep and seemed to probe the soul of those who were being watched by him. This frightened those who dared to confront him. However, that morning he would meet another equal, cold and unable to be intimidated by anyone. Justino got off his horse and went to the big house, where the owner was guarded by some armed thugs to the teeth. Those who accompanied the visitor remained on their horses and, at a distance, skilled snipers were ready for any charge. The two men shook hands, exchanging poisonous looks. They were strangers to each other and had the same suspicion in common. The dialogue took place initially on the part of the newcomer.

— Good morning, I'm Justin, I own a property here near your land, very grateful to have received me

— You are welcome, thanks. But tell me, what is the reason for your visit?

— Yes, I will be brief: A little less than a month ago, some men, who seem to belong to their employees, invaded my property and killed my parents, who were already very old, in cold blood, as well as some of their servants. Not content with this feat, they still set the house on fire with the bodies inside in order to hide the evidence of their actions. So, I came here to identify the criminals and punish them as required by law

— Dear friend, first tell me how you acquired such certainty that it was my employees and who gave you such information?

— And who else has the largest number of thugs in this region?

He learned that one of his slaves had recently fled and the lord hired men from all over the region to go on this search, ordering them to use force and all means to capture and return her. Thus, there is an enormous possibility that some of these hired persons were responsible for this crime.

— And what would lead these men to commit such barbarity with their parents? Were they hiding the slave inside her house or did they help her escape and refused to pass on such information, increasing their anger to the point of attempting against their lives?

— These explanations I cannot provide you. So far what I know, according to what some of my servants have informed me, is that one of their slaves who lived freely used to go to visit them. Her name was Luz. But I'm not sure if she was involved in this story.

Upon hearing such information from the visitor, Dionysus changed his face and it was evident how much he was indignant, but he could not let the investigator attribute the slaughter to his men, shamelessly covering up the truth.

— Luz is one of my sister's servants, Joana, who despite having some perks among the others is not free, but is allowed to walk around the property and sometimes exaggerates, going beyond my lands

— I see, so it is clear that the runaway slave is another?

— Without a doubt. And if the friend believes that his parents did not give the fugitive any shelter, then the terrible act done against them does not come from my men

— Very well, I will continue investigating until I find the culprits. Having a good time

Justino and his companions return to the crime scene and seek more details of the situation with the blacks who lived with their parents and were in the coffee plantations on the day of the massacre, I wanted to understand better how it all happened. Meanwhile, in a plan that was done to eliminate the supposed enemies of the Dantas for good, Dionísio gathered his cronies and ordered an ambush to be carried out to kill the one who dared to interfere in his actions, together with all those who helped him in that investigation.

Men of the worst kind served the orders of the wealthy farmer who did not allow his plans to be interrupted by anyone. His first step in the face of such a situation was to get rid of those who for whatever reason threatened his plans and tried to hinder his evil purposes. Due to the power and wealth that he had.

He felt untouchable and in that arrogance he stepped up with his chin raised on the weakest in strength and financial conditions. Because of his violent temper and the enormous cruelty with which he treated his subordinates, he was regionally known as the worst of the Dantas.

Not even his father, in the times when he dominated his slaves with "iron rods", was seen with such fear and contempt by the other landowners, who hoped that someday somebody would appear with "blood in their eyes" to face the accursed and expel him definitively from that region. And perhaps by divine providence your appeals would be close to being answered. The times of that man's wickedness were over.

Everyone hoped that in some way their rule would be combated with great rigor, especially those who lived under their tyranny. Slaves, subordinates and even family members, like Joana and the unhappy executioner's own mother, dreamed of this moment.

In one of those days a poor slave had been beaten to death by him. What is the crime committed? He simply improperly seized a fruit from the trees in the middle of the plantations in order to kill the hunger that gnawed at his stomach, this attitude cost him his own miserable life after being reported by one of the overseers.

The cruelty of the heir to the dreaded Dantas family was more terrifying than the flames of hell, no one dared to challenge him. That would not be the first or the last of many other barbarities committed by the damned. With the arrival of Luz, the fugitive slave, the level of her anger would reach the highest point of her disrespect for human life. There were only a few minutes left for the sun to hide behind the hills.

When the animals that served as mount for the pursuers of the one that was awaited with great anxiety by the malefactor are harnessed in front of the wide gate of the farm. The journey was long and they all had fatigue marks on their faces, together with the two prisoners who remained tied all the time, back to back, on the backs of a single horse. With the arrival of the thugs in the place, bringing the condemned as a prize after weeks of persecution, a group of surprised and frightened eyes gathered to witness the sad event. Joana, very distressed, went out to meet the slave she created and educated with all her love.

However, she was prevented from embracing her by order of her brother who immediately ordered them to be taken directly to the trunk. The hatred reflected in his eyes and the thirst for revenge drawn in each movement he made it clear that the situation would be terrible.

Especially after being informed by the subordinates that the outsider captured along with the black woman was her defender and helped her escape. Dionysus did not mind that a crowd of other slaves were present there because it was in his interest to carry out the punishment reserved for the fugitive in front of everyone.

The two were brutally dragged to the trunk, where those who rebelled against the authority of the merciless Baron were punished with lashes. They were tied with their bodies glued to a wooden post with their arms raised, attached to a thick rope that wound their swollen, swollen wrists, which forced them to stand. They remained so while the angry executioner descended on his loins the lashes that ripped their sweaty meats from the intense heat of that late afternoon that seemed to happen slowly.

It was a spectacle for everyone who had the courage to watch. However, both the man who whipped the two unfortunates and those in the audience could not hear a single cry of despair coming from his lips. With clenched teeth they endured the pain and did not give them the pleasure of watching them suffer.

Chapter 4 - Back to Captivity

A strong wind started to blow in that darkness that was lit only by the weak light of some fires purposely prepared and lit for that occasion, it seemed that God or some other force of nature was saddened to see the suffering of those innocents.

The most superstitious commented that the spirits rode from side to side in their seven-headed animals promising punishment to the executioners. Fire, sulfur and smoke came out of their nostrils, testifying to the cruelty that was being done there and at the right moment they would punish those responsible for the injustices committed with death.

Black Africans believed and worshiped different types of gods, spirits who lived on another plane and who called Orixás. Totally superstitious, they saw everything in mystery and attributed their fate and destiny to the unknown, they were certain that revenge would fall on the Dantas soon.

The cold of the serene punished even more their bodies exposed in the moonlight and the darkness insisted on taking time to pass, it was hours of humiliation, pain and suffering before the helpless looks of those who, as they were unable to free them from the bonds of the trunk. Their dirty garments and broken by the savagery to which they were subjected were almost useless and their shame was barely seen.

At the mansion, Joana and her mother, as well as the other servants, lamented the deplorable state of the girl who ran around the house and was her most loved and now became a slave condemned to the horrors of the trunk.

He got so caught that his back was in complete disgrace. She remained outside, bound by the arms raised by thick ropes and certainly tired for so long standing, side by side with her failed savior. And who was that black man who came with her? What connection would exist between them so that they deserved the same punishment?

They could not find any other logic than what they claimed to be a couple in love, maybe that was the reason Luz ran away, she would have gone to meet her great love. But, if so, how did you meet? Why did he just appear on the farm?

The worst of all is that these same questions were made by the evil Baron, while drinking a strong dose of cachaça made in one of his many Mills and smoking in an old pipe, but with a good brand. His restlessness made him even more irritated and he whispered small phrases, cursing the day when that unhappy black woman set foot on the farm and enchanted his eyes.

It wasn't just his older brother who had wanted her, he wanted her more than anyone else. The difference is that he had feelings for her, he loved her from the beginning. Terrible thing to even think about, because if such a truth were revealed it would be your greatest shame. How could a man in his position be in love with a black woman? When he heard what his younger brother had done to her, how he raped her, he was indignant. He secretly celebrated his death by blacks in the cane field.

Vengeance was deserved, he was just a child. Despite his rude and fierce manner, he had a strong feeling for her, and he could have supported the attitude taken by his father, in avenging his dishonor, but he needed to maintain the position of authoritarian to continue having everyone under his orders.

The former Baron was always more inclined to the younger son and would have left him all his possessions if he were still alive, so he was relieved that he had been killed.

Alcohol dulled his mind, but it did not prevent his thoughts from taking him far, in a past where his heart had not yet been contaminated by hatred and bitterness. A poor devil, wrapped in his frustrations, his failures and his disappointments.

He had only loved her once in his life, and on top of that she was a black woman, something abhorrent before the eyes of a slavish and prejudiced society. People like himself, prejudiced about the color of their skin and the origin of people. To imagine having dark-skinned children was as terrifying as the intimate union of two males or two females in bed.

He loved her, but he repudiated her offspring from a black woman. That slave, who once saw a child, grew up to be a woman whose physical beauty was the envy of many Portuguese whites at the time. Best of all, it remained there, well within reach. So, he thought, why not have it anyway, by force and without having to give anyone the slightest satisfaction, nor to make any commitment to it? With this absurd idea that she was just one of his many properties, he sexually assaulted her several times, managing to quench his thirst for pleasure in that body he had wanted for years.

But through fate the worst happened. He had no idea that that woman subjected to scorn and violence carried within her a fruit of the abuse she suffered the many times she was forced to satisfy her libidinous impulses.

However, it was almost certain that he would never believe the child to be his if he were born dark-skinned, like the mother. He would claim to be the result of her intimacy with any other black person, including the one who was captured by the thugs. He spent the night awake, filling his lungs with smoke and his stomach with cachaça.

Insomnia prevented him from sleeping and the expectation of seeing a new day be born, where he would again mistreat that disgusting slave who dared to challenge his power made him even more anxious. Finally he saw the light emerging from the mountains and the darkness running at a gallop, the waiting ended, he would return to the point where he stopped. He would use the whip again on the loins of the two convicts.

Outside, the heat that came from the rays of the star King began to warm the cold left by the serene dawn and the two dying woke from a rest tempered by the pain and the burning of the many wounds spread through their bodies.

The drowsiness dissipated completely under the loud sound of the hangman's voice, which returns to the armed place of the whip with which he created wounds whose marks would remain forever, ironing the situation.

— Wake up, you bastards, get ready for breakfast!

New lashes were delivered on the injured flesh of prisoners who no longer had the strength to express the pain they felt. The leader of the thugs, by the name of Barnabas, was ordered by the boss to issue ten lashes to the slave and thirty-nine to his partner, which he did with great pleasure.

They laughed at the misfortune that befell the couple and were amused by that scene of cowardice and the most complete lack of humanity. The pleasure of evil was part of their nature and they were guided by hatred against their fellow men, even those who owed them no insult. Then the order was to remove the black woman from the trunk and take her to the big house, where other women would take care of her injuries. At first, Dionysus did not intend to beat the fugitive to death, only to punish her for daring.

As for Florencio, he had other plans. After being lashed on his loins, the lashes that were determined by the merciless farmer took him to one of the many shacks, where sugar canes and sacks of coffee were stored.

There he was tied again, hoisted by the arms by means of ropes, remaining standing while half a dozen bad elements beat him with kicks and kicks. Florêncio was a man of beautiful stature, he had strong arms and an iron health, however, that whole marathon of beatings would only leave deep marks on his body, but certainly they would not lead him to death. His mouth and nose were bleeding after many punches, his eyes equally swollen made it difficult to see in that place of poor visibility.

While Luz was supported by Joana, Alabá and the other servants of the big house, he remained being tortured. The feared Baron from Coffee, as he liked to be called, approached the black man who was tied up, helpless and in tatters. He orders a truce to be given and for a short time the beating section gives a pause to start an interrogation, Dionísio wanted to know what connection existed between the stranger and his slave.

— Tell me, you bastard, where you met her! What is the type of relationship that exists between you?

The prisoner, despite knowing that his life was worthless to his enemy, dared to confront him nonetheless.

— Go to hell, you bastard!

Florencio's reply deeply irritated his interlocutor, who punched his face several times, leaving him almost faint.

— Miserable! You are wrong to think that you will be able to face me with your ironies, I will get all the answers I want, even if for that it is necessary to remove your skin in life!

Even with his mouth full of blood, the audacious man once again made fun of the dreaded slavery, spitting on his face.

— Hit like a girl, there's no male strength in your fists!

The hateful Baron slaps his face and angrily shouts.

— Keep beating this unfortunate man and don't stop until I order!

The farmer leaves the enclosure and a sequence of new punches and kicks is restarted on the black man who minutes before dared to undo the power of his opponent. Sometime later, Dionysus comes back and starts the interrogation again, but because of the beating, the prisoner does not support and passes out, so he is then awakened by a bucket of cold water, returning to consciousness even though he is still stunned.

With his breathing difficult, his eyes almost completely closed because they had been severely beaten, he was no longer standing on his own legs, the weight of his body was supported only by the thick ropes that held him by the wrists. The enemy positioned himself before him, starting to question him again.

— So, did you decide to collaborate or do you prefer a few more hours of torture to lessen the arrogance?

Florencio was a black man who, despite the color of his skin, was nothing foolish, he knew when to act prudently with his opponent. Then he shot him with words to hit him directly at his weakest point. Almost whispering reveals to his oppressor something he would never have thought was happening.

— She's expecting your child ... Damn you!

Dionysus understood the Negro's whisper perfectly, but he didn't want to believe it, and insisted:

— What did you say, you black devil? Repeat!

Florencio's physical state was to feel sorry for him, he felt as if a train had passed over his body and he had little strength left, which was difficult until he stammered a few words.

. — She's pregnant ... Expect your child, scoundrel!

The man walks away for a few seconds towards one of the four corners of the shack, holding his chin with one hand, looking quite surprised by that revelation. But his pride speaks louder and refuses to consider such a possibility.

— You're lying! If that bitch is expecting a child it can only be yours, damn black man! Surely they had been sneaking around long before she fled my land, now they come back with this conversation. Did you plan to throw that blame on my shoulders, you rascal? What was the purpose? Extort me? Do you want to take over my land? You imbeciles, I will never be the father of a damn black man!

In the impulse of his revolt, he kicks the opponent's face with immense violence, which collapses and loses consciousness again. With the air of a convict, he orders his subordinates to leave and leave the prisoner hanging by the ropes to meet with death.

Back at his quarters, he fills his glass with the strong cachaça extracted from the sugar cane mill, and begins to burn the raw smoke harvested from his own plantations. With each sip of the drink, he followed a drag on his cedar pipe. His thoughts raced through his heavy conscience and suddenly a feeling of guilt started to torment him.

Was it true what the poor devil in captivity said? Wouldn't I have screwed up after being so beaten? Would he not have been delirious after taking dozens of blows to the head and the lashes applied to his loins on the torso? Who knows. The truth is that that revelation disturbed even his soul.

What would they say about him if everything was true? Certainly all other landowners would ridicule the highly respected "Baron of Coffee". They would laugh at him, he would become a laughing stock for his opponents. He couldn't let his family's dreaded name, formed over his father's legacy, be muddled with such shame.

Such news about him would be immensely shameful and would be reported by word of mouth, especially by those who declared themselves their opponents, who disagreed with the way he conducted his empire, with a strong arm and in a merciless manner. Surely they would wonder how a man who was so superior to others ended up in bed with a slave. Faced with such a scandal, the despicable Baron shuddered at the base and understood that he should prevent such news from being made public. And the only way to avoid such a thing was to root out evil, that is.

To kill those who could reveal their error. So the next morning, he went to one of his subordinates and ordered them to punch the black man again who served as threats. If he was still alive after the beatings, he was thrown into the river that drained less than a kilometer from the farm. Florencio had taken a heavy beating from the thugs the night before, but he still survived after the martyrdom. However, if he suffered another similar itch, he would not survive, as he was very weak.

And as the Baron expected, after receiving several blows and having considerably worsened his health, the black man fainted for the third time, went out, seemed to be dead. So he was thrown into the waters of the river and taken the case for granted.

But before he was drowned by his enemies, he regained consciousness in time to avoid his tragic end. However, he preferred to continue pretending to be unconscious. This was not the end that fate had reserved for the second most important character in its history and as soon as it is launched in the icy waters of the river, it starts to swim in the bottom.

Striving as best he could to get to the furthest part of where his alleged killers were, and out there to the bank. His survival plan worked, the thugs who launched him to his death return immediately to his place of origin while he remains stretched out on the hot sand, trying to recover.

Due to his excellent health, as he never abused alcohol, tobacco or any other type of thing that would harm his physical form, it would not be difficult to survive that cowardly attack. After a few hours he managed to drag himself from where he was to more distant, out of the sun's sights and taking shelter under a mulberry tree. His body was almost completely crushed by taking so many hits.

ANGÚSTIAS – Romance

He was breathing hard and it was impossible to stand. Only a great miracle would help him to return home and recover from serious injuries. It could be dangerous there, as Dionysus' men already knew the place, but on the other hand, they seriously thought he was dead at the bottom of the river. Therefore, they would never think to go looking for him there.

The biggest problem, at that moment, would be to find a way to return. After a long time lying there and already losing hope that something good would happen in his favor, he hears footsteps and is frightened.

Thinking that it was the men who tried to kill him, he tried to keep himself hidden from view, but it was not about the thugs but about their salvation. It was luck in person that came to the rescue.

Tereza was a young lady who lived nearby, whose husband was a subordinate in the land of the evil Baron, acting as a cowboy. She watched from afar all the judgments that the thugs practiced with the poor boy and decided to prevent his death.

— Take it easy, I'm not your enemy!

— Please help me...

— Yes, I'll do that, but I need to get more help to get him out of here, because I don't have the strength to take him and apparently he can't even stand up

— No, I am very weak and my legs do not obey ...

— Be quiet, don't try to talk, wait while I get someone who can help us

He then holds tight to his delicate wrists and warns:

— Be careful.

If men who think they have killed me realize that I am alive and what they intend to do with their life, they will be in danger

— I know that, don't worry, I know the right person to give us the help we need

The woman hurriedly leaves and returns to the small village, where most of the workers of the immense Dantas farm reside. They are free people, Portuguese with less financial resources than their bosses, coming from Portugal exclusively to provide their services to Barons and Colonels, farmers and coffee growers.

Juarez was her husband, a kind and hardworking man, averse to his boss's criminal attitudes, however, he served him with dedication because he needed to support the family. That Sunday was his day off given once a month at his boss's own will and on those occasions he dedicated himself to doing some household chores. Tereza arrives in a hurry and he tries to understand the reason for his wife's agony.

— What happened, woman, why all this hurry?

— We need to talk!

— Yes, tell me what happened!

— There's a man lying on the banks of the beaten river and on the verge of death, we have to help him

— But who is this man, how did you find him?

— I was, as usual, picking some fruits in the forest and saw everything. The Baron's thugs brought the poor man bent over a horse and then dragged him to the side of the river, throwing him into the waters.

At first I thought he was dead, but as the criminals left soon I went down the bank in the hope that he would survive and as I thought he did escape

— Woman, you know how merciless the boss is, if you find out that this man is alive and that we are providing him with some kind of help you can punish us in the worst possible way

— My husband we are Christians, we believe in God and in his mercy. Therefore, we cannot allow that poor creature to die without our due assistance. If I witnessed his suffering and after surviving I was the only person to find him, it is because it is up to me, or to us, to help him

Juarez was a religious man, his faith in divine mercy and God's punishment on those who acted indifferently in the face of the needs of others motivated him to always do good.

So, without wasting time, he decided to cooperate with Teresa in favor of the dying man. The two managed, with great effort, to put the wounded in a cart and take him to the house where they lived, from then on she started to take care of his injuries.

At the Dantas farm, the men confirmed to Dionísio the success obtained in the death of the stranger, because he fully relied on the efficiency of his subordinates, the Baron was relieved to know that part of his problems were solved. He was reassured that the captured slave's companion knew about her possible pregnancy and that he would be the father.

As much as I thought that idea was absurd, I could not run the risk that such information would leak and reach the popular ears. But the other threat still had to be dealt with, and after much thought, he concluded that the best thing to do would be to order his men to possess the slave sexually.

That way there would be no chance of being attributed to him that pregnancy, despite the fact that she was already pregnant. if she was pregnant for more than a month, the plan could work. In this way he ordered her to be removed from the mansion and taken back to the trunk, where she was flogged again with whips, then the thugs took her to one of the many shacks and there raped her, there were ten in such a monstrosity made.

Joana and the other women of Casa Grande only heard the screams of the black woman who was brutally raped by men who seemed possessed by the devil himself, without being able to do anything to free her from such barbarity. Then, after each of the ten elements completely overcome by the thirst for sex has grown tired of that infamous act, they take it back to the trunk and another sequence of lashes is given.

After having created all that staging in order to mask his secret, Dionísio orders that the slave be returned to her sister and the other women so that her wounds are treated. Luz stayed in the farmhouse for several weeks, being cared for by Joana, Alabá and other servants.

It happened that due to the violence with which she was raped by the thugs and the immense beating she took during her time in the trunk, she ended up being the victim of a serious hemorrhage that the women could not contain. Informed by his sister that the slave was at risk of death, the Baron sent for the doctor in the city to help her.

However, the place was distant and even with all the effort to get to the farm as soon as possible it was impossible to avoid the worst, after spilling a lot of blood came to lose the child that was already developing in its womb. The doctor explained the fact to Joana and as soon as Luz became fully aware, she was informed of the event, receiving the information very naturally.

This left women perplexed by the indifference of that mother not to be saddened by having lost her fetus. Being the two alone, Lucinete and her protector talked a lot about the situation, from the flight of the black woman to her return to the farm, her trip to the trunk with her partner until that moment when they were talking. Joana, like everyone else there, believed that the pregnancy was the result of an intimate relationship between her and the Negro with whom she was found. It was up to the young woman to explain to her godmother what had actually happened.

— It wasn't his, Mrs.

— Do not call me that, you are more than a simple servant for me in this house, always call me a godmother, as I taught you since I was little

— Yes, sorry godmother ...

— And how, then, was the child you were expecting not from that boy with whom you were found? Did you happen to lie around with several men, my daughter?

— God forbid, godmother, I'm no slut!

— Well, then explain this story to me better. If the child was not the man you decided to leave and run from, who would it be?

— First I want you to know that it was not for him that I ran away from the farm

— Oh no? And why was it, then?

— It's a long story, but I'll let you know ...

Luz went on to explain everything that happened to her, since the abuses suffered almost daily by Dionísio.

Her struggles, persecutions and torments she had to face during her time away and how Florencio helped her, Martim death, when they were approached by the thugs and brought back to the farm. Aware of the whole story, Joana felt disgusted at bringing the same blood of the monster that was said to be her brother in her veins, she did not understand why she was so different from him and her father, another plague that when she died she did not miss anyone. .

Outraged, she thought of going to Dionysus to confront him, but she was prevented by the requests of Luz that convinced her that it was useless to take that kind of action and that would only ignite the wrath of the damned on herself. He was just a woman, wanting to expose his brother to the consequences of his mistakes, but without any power to convince him of his evils.

The young woman's arguments convinced her protector to act with greater caution, she would think better and only then would she see how she could help Luz stay free from the clutches of the terrible murderer. In the days that had passed, he never left his feet in the room where the girl was recovering, he feared that his brother would cause him some harm and even though he knew he would not be able to stop him, he chose to remain alert.

Without anyone knowing, he armed himself with a pistol that he had kept in his belongings for a long time, he knew how to use it because he learned in his adolescence with someone he once loved, but was no longer there to support her, a sad story that a day lived long ago, during his youth. Joana was not a calm and submissive woman, but she had already been rebellious and responsible for major conflicts in the Dantas family. Despite not being compared to the evil character of the two brothers.

ANGÚSTIAS – Romance

She seriously fought against the authoritarian dictates of her father, who saw women as inferior to men and that their use was only to marry and bear children. Prejudiced ideology of the time. So he decided to live a great and mind-boggling passion with a man of lower social class, arousing the ire of the then Baron who ordered his men to kill the individual and kept the rebellious girl in private prison for several months.

No right to even go out in the yard or communicate with anyone other than the mother. It happened that, during this period of extravagance, Joana not only managed to defy her father's authority and conquer his contempt, but also threw away her own honor as a woman, which in those days was considered a horrible thing to do.

From then on it was impossible to get a marriage candidate, since no boy wanted to have her as a wife after what happened, he became poorly spoken and synonymous with shame in the eyes of the important families of his time.

That was the reason why she remained alone for a lifetime, did not get married or had her own home. Dionísio was another who had no descendants and would have no one to leave his property to after his death, his only passion was a black woman who could not take on as a wife because of the difference in social class, color and race. A nobleman could not join a slave, he would be seen as a sacrilege before the church and all eyes of society.

Therefore, as far as one could see, the Dantas lineage was doomed to end. Upon being informed of Jerônimo's death, through one of the servants, Joana passed the information on to Luz, who mourned her friend for several days. He had been vitally important in his life, especially during his flight, when he was struggling to escape the oppression of one who had sexually abused him for a long time.

However, what she did not know was that in fact he was rescued from death by two charitable souls. He was not far from there, recovering from the serious injuries resulting from the terrible beatings he suffered while he remained a prisoner of the Dionysus thugs.

Divine providence saw to it that he was rescued and survived so that in the end justice would be done. In this way his recovery advanced in a surprising way and soon he would rise up against the greatest representative of the Dantas, who cowardly decided for the undue punishment of those who only wanted to put justice into practice in favor of an innocent person.

Florencio, despite not declaring himself openly, fell in love with the new friend whom he decided to protect with his own life and it was wrong for anyone who thought that after such injustice he would simply recover and then return to his property without returning the his oppressors a duplicate balance of the affronts he suffered, for if there was one thing he did not usually let go of, it was undeserved humiliation.

Dionísio Dantas and his thugs who were preparing to live a real hell. They messed with the wrong man, it would be better if they were buried alive, because the revenge on them would be terrible.

Florencio's recovery took place after a few weeks and the truth about having escaped alive from the attack he suffered from the thugs remained confidential. With his health restored, he would find a place of refuge and from there he would create a strategy for revenge against the abominable Baron and his men.

She remembered that Luz had commented on the elderly couple who helped her escape and decided to go to them to see if she could get any help. However, when he arrived there, he came across Justin and his men.

Being aware of everything that happened to Benedita and Ambrósio, as well as the cowardly way in which they were killed. The two men came to have enemies in common and devised a plan to destroy the Baron, free Luz and bring peace to that region.

It turns out that it would take a strong army of well-armed men to do that, and the soldiers who accompanied Justino on his return to his homeland had already returned to the capital. well a weapon, so what could they do against more than a hundred experienced thugs?

If they were defeated, it would be better if they ended up dead or otherwise a terrible martyrdom awaited them on the trunks of the Dantas. Florencio himself had already experienced the painful taste of the whip. Talking to Dionysus was a complete waste of time, a direct confrontation would be suicide.

So what was left to do was to quietly enter the farm and take Luz out of there, setting everything on fire to distract the thugs and thus carry out the rescue safely. This would certainly cause damage to the Baron, as he would lose part of his assets. And then, knowing that the slave was taken from her property right under her nose would be a damned affront to that son of darkness, capable of making him neigh with hatred. That was Florencio's initial idea.

However, Justino, who was almost absolutely sure of the connection between the evil slave and the death of his parents, would not be content with just burning part of the enemy's property and stealing the black woman from him, wanted to punish him more severely. That way, he would add more poison to the plate of cold food that the bastard would eat.

Chapter 5 - The Invasion

After gathering some of his servants, the most manly and willing to fight, they devised a surprise attack scheme against the farmer, but there was still something to be done to make everything work as well as possible. Luz should be informed about what would happen, in order to be prepared to make the escape together with her rescuers.

Here is the biggest problem, how to warn her? The way would be to pass the message on to him through one of the servants of the big house. Alabá would be the most suitable person, however, how to locate her to send a ticket with the information to Luz? Vicente, one of the blacks who knew the maid, explained that at least once a month some of those who served the women of the Dantas family were sent to the village to buy products from the province, and it would be a great opportunity to talk to the maid. that would certainly be among them.

By coincidence, the next morning would be the exact day in question and what should be done was just go to the village to pass the message on to the black woman, who would certainly pass it on to Lucinete. And so it was done. Alabá and five others went to make the usual purchases at the behest of Mrs. since the products from the province could not be lacking in the house.

ANGÚSTIAS – Romance

The person who entered the scene to deliver the black woman the note, containing the details about the plan of the two men, was Vicente himself, explaining that Jerônimo was alive and that this information should be passed on to Luz, in order to be attentive. Alabá returned to the farm and without anyone noticing the friend received the information received.

— My God, how relieved I am to know that Jerome is not dead! Did you see him in person?

— No, Vicente was the one who sent me this letter and informed you about the news

— You did well, my friend, I'll be waiting for him

— Luz, you need to get away from here as soon as possible, because as soon as that bastard realizes he is recovered he will do the same things as before

— I know that, Alabá, I will never again be sexually abused by that monster

— So be prepared my friend, this morning they will come to get you out of here

Luz loved Joanna like a mother and decided to hide nothing from her, so she could let him know everything.

— So you plan to leave again, my daughter?

— Yes, godmother, it must be so

— I understand, my child, I know that your stay here will not bring you good results. My brother seems to have lost his mind and acts like a fool capable of committing the greatest absurdities.

Run away, my girl, defend your life that walks by a thread!

— It will be tonight, godmother, please take care and don't challenge your brother

— So that God and Our Lady of Grace can accompany you on this journey and make you very happy. Try not to be caught again by the thugs because your punishment will be worse than the one suffered in the trunk, Dionísio may even kill you!

— That unfortunate person will only put his hands on me again if it is after he is dead

— So come here, give me a big hug

— I thank you for all the good you did for me, the education and the love you gave me, your kindness to me will never be forgotten

— No need to thank, your presence in my life just did me good. Be happy my girl

Their conversation took place inside one of Casa Grande's several rooms, but they were not smart enough to avoid being overheard. That's because Joana trusted the servants she kept inside the mansion, she believed that none of them would use falsehood, because she always treated them with great affection and respect.

He never saw them as slaves, but as equals. However, bad people exist in all social classes, from the rich to the poor, from the free to the slave. Rosa, one of the black women who helped with domestic services, heard the whole story and decided to tell one of the thugs who surrounded her there, with whom she kept a romance on the sly.

She was tremendously disrespected for the way her Mrs. treated Luz, since she didn't even have white skin, she was black like any other, but she had privileges. He gossiped in order to cause great disgrace in the life of the one he envied.

The thugs immediately took the information to the boss who, without wasting time, ordered an ambush to be prepared to surprise the invaders, spreading well-armed men throughout the property, with the mission of capturing them alive if possible, as he wanted to give them all the worst of the punishments.

Jerônimo and Justino, together with ten other blacks who were willing to help them, left for the Dantas farm that night, not knowing for sure what their fate was in store for.

Luz said goodbye to the two people she learned to love deeply in that place, her godmother Joana and Alabá, the best and only friend. The bedroom window that was on the outside of the big house remained half-open, waiting for her friends to arrive to take her away.

She did not prepare luggage or wear the clothes of many fabrics, as was usual, but a simple dress without many combinations, dark in color to be discreet in the moonlight.

However, to her surprise, suddenly the room was invaded by Dionisio's men who gagged her, then took her to a place far away from there. It did no good to fight in order to free himself from the hands of his opponents, because they were individuals endowed with an extraordinary force, accustomed to dominating their victims. At that very moment, while the girl was overpowered and taken to another point on the farm, the siege closed.

Other thugs were located in strategic places waiting for the invaders. Justino, in the company of ten other companions, entered the property in the certainty that they were not being observed, heading towards the barracks in order to set them on fire, as it was part of the plan to cause distraction while Florêncio rescued Luz.

A white cloth was purposely placed on the window of the room where she was going to be, but what would serve as an indication for him to find her became a trap.

There she would be faced with a terrible surprise, because instead of her friend she would find enemies ready to dominate him. The Baron's orders were to deliver him alive. Without a shadow of a doubt the worst awaited him.

On the other hand, those who intended to set the barracks on fire did not even light a match and even found themselves surrounded by thugs. After receiving the warning to surrender, they did not show any reaction and soon freaked out because they were unarmed. They were taken by surprise and taken to the presence of Dionísio, who was anxiously awaiting the outcome of the event, nor did he close his eyes all the way through the night waiting for news.

Justin and the ten blacks were easily surprised and dominated, now they would be martyred to death under the whip of the worst evil character they ever had the chance to meet. The Baron was surprised to find his neighbor among the prisoners.

— Now look who we have here, if it is not the stranger who visited me days ago. Apparently your credentials have fallen a lot, mate. He went from someone apparently important to a leader of vandals!

Before he was accompanied by military men and now by a band of filthy blacks

— Murderer, I know it was you who ordered that massacre that culminated in the death of my parents, you will still pay dearly for that, scoundrel!

— You can shout as much as you want, you unfortunate, now he is just a poor devil who will regret immensely for daring to invade my property, he will wish he had never been born!

— It is good that I put an end to once in my life, damn you, otherwise I swear you will pay a high price for all the harm you have done against these innocent people all this time!

— Take this wretch from here and put him trapped in one of the logs to watch the show, because today I will have fun like never before!

All the prisoners were taken to the place he had chosen for the punishment he felt necessary to apply to the invaders on his property. First, he would punish the poor blacks who chose to help Florencio and Justino with the flawed plan to rescue the slave.

His evil purpose was to judge as much as possible with the poor in sight of the opponent, in order to martyr him and in a way show his power, after he had his fury satisfied he would kill them and turn to the opponent, delighting in going down whip your loins and tear your hides until all the blood drains from your veins.

There the faithful copy of the devil and all the evil of darkness could be seen in one individual, without any positive influence of good. His pleasure was in doing evil in all its patterns and aspects. He delighted in spreading the wickedness in the lives of innocents and turning them into his fatal victims.

His contentment was in killing and destroying his opponents, guilty or not, he was of little interest. Each of the blacks caught in the episode were tied to the trunks and started to be whipped by the wicked farmer. Justin was placed in a privileged position, facing the horror show and it was possible for him to watch everything that happened with his companions.

Her cries of pain echoed through the forest around the farm and she was heard by the other slaves who, from their shacks, were terrified to hear their cries. They listened in fright to the martyrdom experienced by those who dared to challenge their master, that would serve as an example so that they would not have the absurd idea of practicing the same mistake. This was Dionysus's main objective.

As he promised, the wicked Baron judged as much as he wanted from the blacks and had fun with the whip on his loins for several hours, until he fainted from suffering. Then he ordered his underlings to light the fire that he had previously prepared to prepare.

In order to complete his ruthless act, he threw the blacks still alive in the fire that licked the highest parts of the place. That macabre scene made Justin tremble at the base, as he understood that this would surely be his end, but that was not the end that fate had in store for him.

While living that hell his future was planned in a way opposite to reality by the writer of life. Throughout that process, Dionysus trusted that his men would be fully carrying out their orders and that they would surprise the invaders who intended to rescue Luz. Yes, he would be correct to think that way if things had not gone differently than planned. In addition to having the support of Justino and the other blacks, Florencio sought help from his newest friends, Tereza and Juarez.

Who saved him from death after the attack he suffered and was thrown into the river. During the rescue, with the support of other supporters of the cause, they went to the vicinity of the mansion and dominated the guards. After being properly dominated, the liberator of the helpless slave comes into action. Luz is finally free from the clutches of her oppressors and flees far from the prison where she had been placed.

During the escape, passing through the undergrowth he met on the way before reaching the exit of the immense property, it was still possible to hear the desperate screams of the poor devils who helped Justino before they were burned, under the wrath of the tyrant.

In the distance, it was possible to hear the crack of the whip that crumbled their bodies and spilled blood from their veins, stealing their lives. Luz understood that it didn't matter if someone was pious and tried to give a black man the dignity he deserved as a human being, there would always be someone willing to deny them respect. She was raised and educated by Joana after the death of her parents, she could have a different life, be happy, but this was not allowed because she had dark skin. Those poor devils were being beaten to death by Dionysus for being black.

Even if they were caught invading their property, if they were white they would receive a more dignified, faster death. A shot in the center of the forehead or a hanging like cattle thieves. But no, they were black and because of their color they deserved the most terrible punishment. The worst of it was to remember that Justin also had dark skin.

Certainly and the treatment with him would be no different, but Florencio intended to rescue his friend, would not allow him to be killed by the evil Baron.

For this purpose, the two traveled through the night into the forest in the most complete darkness and full of dangers to prevent them from being chased and arrested by the thugs, as happened the other time, stopping the long journey only when they arrived at Florêncio's property, where, after taking only what was necessary left for the municipality of Field, Waterfall with the prospect of asking the emperor, Justino's friend, to send a battalion of men to free him from the clutches of the evildoer Dionísio, before he was killed.

The house remained intact, the criminals took nothing and no one invaded it. So, they prepared two of the best horses, got enough food for the trip and galloped on, as time acted against the life of the imprisoned friend. Everything had to be done in a hurry, so the spurs hit the animals and made them run as fast as possible.

The distance was long, but the desire and need to achieve that goal was greater. On the farm, Florencio relied only on divine providence. He was beaten by the thugs, tied to one of the trunks and had to watch from the box the cruel death of his friends who, after being terribly tortured in the trunk, were thrown alive in the burning fire. Dionysus, like his father, had this abominable practice as a habit.

The taste of victory was sweet in the mouth of the merciless Dantas, so he chose to postpone the death of his last and most important prisoner until the following night in order to further increase the fear that his subordinates and other landowners had of him.

Everyone trembled at his enormous evil. So he ordered some of his servants to spread an invitation to his neighbors to attend a large party that he would hold on his property.

He knew that no one would dare to disappoint him, all the guests would be present, regardless of whether the party was pleasant or not. An expansive number of guests were invited to attend the event. Immense dread was felt by all the slaves and the women in the mansion.

Gradually, in the late afternoon of that Saturday, dozens of people arrived at the farm and were received by the evil Baron who thanked the presence of his guests as if in fact he needed such a formality, because in reality what sent them was not an invitation, but a subpoena. Whoever dared not to attend would end up dead or have his goods consumed by fire, the ordinary would not forgive the affront.

Much drink was distributed, meat at will, music and dance. And woe to anyone who was unwilling not to have fun or enjoy the joy of the festivities promoted with the sole objective of at the end executing before the terrified looks of those present those who declared themselves the enemy of the most feared man in the region.

Nobody wasted time imagining that suddenly the evil Baron had become nice and decided to throw a party for his neighbors, there was something macabre hidden behind everything there, that was what everyone expected from the beginning.

The search for help made by the two happened quietly, because until then Dionísio and his thugs were entertained with the martyrdom of the blacks and the alleged death of Justin that would happen in the form of a show.

However, when the most macabre moment of that crazy party approached, the demonized farmer ordered that the one who for a long time sexually abused was brought to the party so that she could see what he was capable of against the US and positioned themselves as his enemies.

Until that moment, the merciless slave master still had no idea that Florencio had already successfully implemented his plan to free the slave and that the two were far away. When the one who was tasked with bringing the black woman to his presence reported that all the men who were placed to prevent her rescue by the invaders were unconscious and she fled, Dionísio was very angry and soon ordered the incompetents to be executed by the bullet. rifle, including the one that brought you the disappointing news.

He immediately selected several of his most valiant men and sent them in search of the fugitive with the express order to bring her back alive or dead. Disgusted with the situation, he expelled all the guests from the party he prepared with the intention of hosting a great show and retired to his rooms, where he would drink cachaça and smoke his pipe until he saw his thugs arriving with his slave.

Fortunately, he realized the situation too late and as much as the thugs had made long searches throughout the entire length of the property and even in the same places where they had followed him, it was all in vain. In the frustration of not being able to find her, they set fire to Florencio's house and destroyed all of her property. On the property of Justin, they oppressed the blacks who were there and killed some of those who tried to react in their own or family's defense. Finally, they returned empty-handed.

In that same period of time Luz and Florêncio arrived at the municipality of Field, Waterfall at daybreak, asked for information and soon found themselves in front of the Emperor's residence, a close friend of the man who was a prisoner in the lands of the Dantas, being threatened with death. After explaining all the tragedy that occurred, from the abuses of Dionysus towards the slave, his escape and the persecutions he suffered.

ANGÚSTIAS – Romance

His meeting with Justino and the plan to remove Luz from the farm, which culminated in his capture and in the death of the ten blacks who accompanied him ... So the Emperor decided to resend about one hundred and fifty armed men to the teeth to free his friend before the worst happened.

Everything would be done in secrecy, no one but those involved in that conversation should be aware of the plan. What Dionysus did not know was that his prisoner was an extremely valuable merchant in his city and that he had a strong influence among the great names of society, including other counts, colonels and even the Emperor himself. He actively participated in the provincial activities and became a reference among those who rendered services to royalty.

Thus it was a terrible mistake to imprison and flog him as if he were a mere slave, for now he would have to account for his actions to people above his power. The arrival of one hundred and fifty soldiers to the lands of the Dantas took place immediately after the order given by the highest authority in the province and together with them came Florêncio, because he felt the duty to give back to his new friend the freedom that he lost because of him.

Soon the platoon sent on the mission was already assembled on the property in order to free the man who was being held captive by the Baron, setting goals to rescue him. The initial idea was that a messenger should be sent to Dionysus, bringing to him a document signed by the Emperor's own hand, ordering the immediate release of the prisoner.

Demanding, too, that from that day on, stop walking in the wake of slave Lucinete. Since she would now belong to the empire that would take care of her entire protection. If he passively accepted the orders he would avoid a terrible confrontation with the officers.

Otherwise the commander of the cavalry sent was authorized to invade his lands and release the prisoner. The messenger galloped off towards the farm and there he asked to speak personally with the farmer, then passing the letter duly signed and sealed by the emperor to the disgusting man who read it and showed contempt for the request made by the authority.

As an immediate answer, he drew his weapon and fired three times at the news bearer, who fell lifeless right there at the feet of his mount. Dionysus then ordered some of his people to end the body and prepare for a possible attack.

The thugs, which were far fewer than the platoon sent by the emperor, were in a position of defense and attack waiting for the military that could appear at any moment. After not counting on the return of the messenger, understanding that he would have been killed, the commander authorized the attack on the property of the arrogant Baron. The platoon of military and Florencio set out to fight a bloody battle against the enemy.

Still about two hundred meters away, they left their mounts behind and went on foot. They spread throughout the surrounding forest and the thugs were waiting for them. As soon as they realized the advance of the military, they took the lead and fired on the invaders, who immediately retaliated. The boom of shots fired by large-caliber weapons sounded like an echo and bullets tinkled through the trees, tearing the tranquility of the place.

Little by little the armed force advanced and many of Dionysus' men fell to the ground. They were not countering ordinary snipers, they were men properly trained in the art of war and they knew the strategy of facing an enemy in battle like never before. Every ten shots fired in the direction of the farm, at least five hit the thugs directly.

ANGÚSTIAS – Romance

The unfortunate ones who served as a barrier between the vigilantes and the accursed slavery who were hidden all the time inside their chambers were waiting, waiting for the final result of the battle. While the war between soldiers and thugs was fought at the cost of spilling a lot of blood, Florencio went in the opposite direction, looking for a way to get to the place where his friend was.

He was in agony without eating or drinking for many days, stuck to the trunk and near death. Only two individuals were watching the wretch and they were shot. Then, after releasing Justin, he had to drag him away from the scene, using all the strength he possessed.

The man, completely malnourished and with his body washed in blood, due to the beating suffered the night before, when he was once again beaten under the wrath of Dionysus's whip, could not even babble. Forcibly he spoke some disconnected words, much less stand up. Even so, after much effort it was possible to withdraw from there to a safe place.

Back on the farm, without being noticed, Florencio seizes a cart that was abandoned on the ground and used it to take the wounded farther from the battlefield. Justin was taken by his friend to the couple's home who helped him recover after being savagely beaten by the Baron's men and thrown into the river.

There he was healed of his wounds and fed properly, soon his health would be restored. After rescuing and putting his friend to safety, Florencio wastes no more time and returns to help his companions in the fight against the merciless slavery in an attempt to get his hands on him and make him pay for all his crimes. The armed struggle continued outside and inside the mansion the women hid in fear even under their beds.

Afraid of being victims of a stray bullet. Joana and her mother, together with the maids, were terrified. Her brother's monster, responsible for all that situation, did not seem to care about their safety in the midst of that shooting from hell and continued to stay in their rooms in the greatest tranquility, smoking the damn pipe and drinking cachaça from the mill.

In the middle of calm, as if nothing terrible was happening outside, the foolish farmer remained oblivious to the bloodbath he caused. Of the more than one hundred men who defended their property with their lives, dozens had already been killed. They were like obedient dogs and capable of giving their lives in exchange for their protection. Poor devils!

Far away from there, Luz, who remained in Field, Waterfall, was apprehensive about the result of the plan made in order to free Justino, as he had no way of knowing how things were going. Her anxiety was so great that not even the words of comfort she received from the Countess calmed her and her intention was to ride towards where they could be. In fact, she learned to care about her new friend, she was fond of him and sometimes believed that a strong feeling was growing inside her.

She felt strange about that. Never before had he lived a passion, nor could he imagine himself living a great love, but lately his heart was racing whenever they were close to each other. She knew sex violently and was disgusted by men until she found herself being treated with such affection and cared for by Florêncio, from the day they met when they arrived at her house, during the escape from Dionísio's clutches. The sacrifices made by the boy to free her from private prison impressed her. He put himself in danger, invading the farm, risking his life just to rescue her, this could not go unnoticed by the girl who never had anyone who gave him such value before.

ANGÚSTIAS – Romance

Besides her godmother, Joana. So, his anguish at being distant and without news was understandable. Thus, his decision to return to the lands of the Dantas in search of the one who seemed to have won his heart became inevitable.

However, the Emperor decided to send in his company another squadron of military personnel to guard his trip and help those found in battle. The return trip took almost two days on horseback to the place of the fight, but neither she nor the others felt unwell. Still in the distance, it was possible to hear the sounds of shots fired by those who sacrificed their lives, some for the freedom of the innocent and others in defense of evil.

Until that moment, the men who fought for Dionysus had lost many men and were almost unable to gain victory over the military who resisted the attack with greater advantage. And to the surprise of the enemies who still thought they could overcome the brave defenders of justice, new military men joined those who courageously struggled to resist the battle and retreated under a heavy rain of heavy lead.

In this second phase of the fight even the young slave entered the armed struggle and made use of what she learned from her old friend, Martim, murdered some time ago, fighting back the enemies' insults.

She, however, knew that at that time of the championship her godmother Joana and her friend Alabá would be at the mercy of that carnage and needed to remove her from the mansion, before the wretch decided to do any harm against them, since their cowardice had no limits.

So, with the help of Florêncio, who was immensely happy to see her mainly in the company of an even greater number of combatants, he went to rescue the women.

The thugs were not even aware of the action of the couple who entered through an area far from the place of the battle and reached the back door of the mansion. Thus it was possible to locate the women whom they tried to remove from that place where death was pacing from side to side. Due to the advanced age of her mother and herself, Joana chose to stay in the big house, because she feared the worst outside

. — Sorry, my daughter, I know your intentions are the best for me, but mom and I are already old enough to live this kind of adventure, we prefer to stay here and hope to God that nothing bad will happen to us

— But godmother, the risk of becoming fatal victims of this crazy war is immense, come with me to be safe, we have some friends who can give you shelter at least while this situation is resolved

— We are very grateful for worrying about us, my daughter, but Joana is absolutely right, we are not old enough to run away in the forest, we would only hinder you

— Mrs. please understand, I will not be at peace if you stay here!

— Take Alabá with you, help her in our place

— But, godmother ...

— Obey me, Luz, don't argue!

— Okay, I'll do as you ask, but please take care

Luz, Alabá and Florêncio leave after receiving a tight hug from Joana and her mother. The three undertake a flight to the woods and the two women are taken to a safe place until the armed struggle between the military and the thugs ends.

The battle continued in a frightening way, the thugs fell to the ground like flies. Only after one of his subordinates warned him that they were completely defeated by the military who worked in defense of Justin, did Dionysus decide to act in his own defense. But contrary to what everyone might expect, the coward made an escape in the opposite direction of the battle, escaping on a mount properly prepared for the deserter.

In the company of four thugs he escaped without being seen by those who wanted to punish him. However, the order given by the Emperor was that he be arrested and taken to the province to be tried and sentenced to hang. He was aware of this, knew that he went beyond what he could and would be hanged for defying Imperial authority.

That way he understood that if his men were losing the battle, the ideal would be to escape while he could. Therefore, his plan was to proceed towards the North, there he would find refuge in the lands of some of those fond of him and his evil methods, were colonels who practiced the same injustices and treated his slaves under the weight of the whip, in addition to other infamous customs.

In his view there he would be safe and away from the punishment that awaited him, however, that was not what would be reserved for the damned. Their evils would be charged under the strong pulse of the law. Reduced to a few men, the thugs decided to surrender and the vigilantes dominated the entire property. Justino and Florêncio entered the mansion and announced the victory for the women who were hidden there. The other slaves and their families who also remained hidden inside their shacks, fearing that they would be victimized by a stray bullet, gradually appeared. Frightened and trembling with fear of the invaders.

They fall to their knees in front of the military in respect for the uniform, its currency and the fact of knowing how to recognize their victory. The poor blacks did not know how to behave before the authorities, nor would they remain captive or be killed like most thugs during the fight.

However, Justino and Florêncio gathered the blacks and their families in the immense courtyard in front of the Casa Grande and announced that all of them could remain there, in that land, living in peace and exercising their tasks normally, however, they would no longer be treated as slaves but as brothers.

He himself would start to live on the farm in the company of Luz, as it was his intention to make her his wife. At that moment he takes the opportunity to ask the old slave the usual question.

— But it all depends on her, my friends! So, before all of you, without wasting any more time I want to ask you, my beloved, do you accept to marry me?

She did not hesitate to give the answer that was already written in her affectionate smile.

— Yes, my love, for sure

At that moment, a roar of shouting and applause was heard, from the euphoria of everyone present. It was a great victory with the taste of a job done, all that remains is to locate the damn Baron who escaped unscathed and who was supposed to pay for his crimes, but that would soon happen. After the celebration of the victory achieved against their enemies, Justino and Florêncio, with the cooperation of the commander of the troop formed by the military who survived the battle.

Concluded the task of gathering the bodies of the dead. Then they cremated all the dead over a large fire, as there were so many who lost their lives in the confrontation. Then they galloped off, searching for the now fugitive Dionísio Dantas, wanted by all that region and accused of several crimes, among them the most serious of which was to disobey the direct order of the Emperor.

In the province, the Court decided that he would be hanged as soon as he was arrested to serve as an example to others who, as such, could be practicing the same savagery. The Baron, always accompanied by four gunmen properly armed and ready to defend him with his life, finally arrived at his destination, a vast farm located further north of his former lands. The intention was to stay at a friend's house for a while before restoring his power.

Chapter 6 - The Freedom Prize

The property on which Dionísio and his men just arrived belonged to Colonel Leopoldo, a friend of old times, they met while still young and grew up practicing the same abuses against women and children. Pedophilia, heinous crimes against innocents, disobedience to the authorities and various other barbarities have always been his favorite diversions.

At that time, they were two playboys who believed they had the freedom and the right to do what they thought was best, due to the fact that they belonged to wealthy families, so they spent their entire lives committing countless absurdities. But time passed, each went their own way and stopped visiting each other. However, neither of them changed old habits and continued to abuse their luck.

Dionysus finally came face to face with the donkeys and now he had become a fugitive, pursued by the Empire and his presence was a threat to anyone who intended to help him. As the news that he became a defendant before the Portuguese Crown spread throughout the region, by express orders from the Emperor, Leopoldo was already aware of the news. In this way, avoiding committing himself to such a situation, he closed the doors to the unsuccessful Baron from Coffee.

Seeing that not even a decent place to rest his tired body would have at that moment. Dionísio and his cronies did not even manage to get through the gate and were already sent away. Such was his surprise and disappointment when he heard from a thugs mouth that his boss did not want to receive him, he never thought of going through such humiliation.

And because they wanted to exalt themselves against the messenger, they were surrounded by several others, threatened with death if they insisted on staying there. Having no idea what to do or where to go, he dismissed his men to return, handing them a handful of coins that he carried with them, releasing them from the commitment to escort him.

However, faithful to the boss whom they served for so long, they pledged not to abandon him in that situation until he found a safe place to lay his head, even if they had to confront those who might come after him. From there they went further west, towards the river, where Constância, her closest cousin, lived. This was a woman with a good heart, married to a great cattle rancher, with an abundant life, very religious and helpful.

However, when he arrived there, he found that she was bedridden and very ill, she could not make any decision on how to help him and the husband, aware of what had happened, refused to accommodate him on his property for fear of reprisals from the authorities.

He had nowhere else to go or who to turn to, the way was to surrender or fight to the death against his pursuers. In this way, he left again for lands that were farther and farther away. He became an outsider in the company of his faithful companions and became a looter, stealing and taking over everything that could be sold in order to maintain his survival. Jerônimo, Florêncio and the military spent approximately six months looking for the bandit.

But he only heard about his passages in the villages, practicing thefts and spreading terror everywhere. He and his partners in crime were joined by others, similarly addicted to the criminal life to which he had become accustomed. In a short time the former farmer and slave became the leader of the largest band of criminals and outlaws that were known in those days. Their crimes went beyond all evil previously committed.

The Emperor was informed of the situation and sent several platoons of military personnel in search of outlaws with an order to arrest them at any price. In some cases they came across the group, but were unable to stop the gang despite the exchange of gunfire and the deaths of some of them.

The two friends were summoned to appear in the province, where the Empire raised Florêncio to the position of captain of the military forces and entrusted him to go out looking for troublemakers and put an end to his criminal actions.

The persecution lasted for months and wherever the rebels passed, they caused destruction. They plundered, killed, set fire to everything on the way, abused women, raped virgins, whether they were children, young people or teenagers, no one escaped and those who tried to free their families were tortured and then burned alive.

Finally Dionysus joined his right group of individuals, he felt fulfilled alongside those demons. Sometimes he even claimed that he had never been happier in his life, it was as if he had lived part of his existence in the right place and among the wrong people. Even having owned a cradle of gold, he felt that his destiny was to live there, amid the shadows of evil and in the practice of promiscuity. His character was made of the lowest moral values, while the persecution of Dionysus and his band of rioters continued.

At the Luz farm he had the support of Joana and the other residents to transform the old place of slavery, torture, injustice and suffering into a place of peace, love, justice and prosperity. The blacks who belonged to the Dantas were freed from the weight of the chains and became people who owned their own destiny.

They could leave in search of their paths in life, but they preferred to stay and help the new Mrs. take care of the property. The black woman, who once was just a fugitive slave, was now the new owner of the lands where in the past she saw her parents being burned alive and was sexually abused, persecuted and humiliated.

Joana, her godmother, was the one who should inherit all the assets that for a long time were managed by her older brother, however she did not feel prepared for such responsibility and as she had no children and had no other heirs, she passed on this task to her. Nobody more deserving than she who suffered there the worst affronts and persecutions to continue the name of the Dantas.

Thus, her godmother went with her to the province where the Emperor had already determined that she was a black woman free from the slavery of her former owner and registered her as a daughter, passing on to her all the family assets. Thus, the former slave came to be recognized by all as the first black woman to become officially free and owner of land.

On top of that, as a courtesy of the Crown, due to the influence of Joan and her friendship with Count Justino, she received the honorable title of Countess, further humiliating her enemies and fair-skinned critics. She cared little for those who turned red with anger at seeing that a black woman had received such an honor.

While they, even though they were white, were never equally honored. What really made her happy was that she could help her African brothers to live in peace and without the yoke of slavery. The blacks, now workers, continued to cultivate sugar canes, manufacture cachaça and coffee plantations, but spontaneously and without any fear of the whip of their former white masters.

The friends Tereza and Juarez, who helped Florencio, when he was in agony on the banks of the river and took care of Justino's wounds, assumed the role of chief foreman of the farm and administrator of the servants in the mansion, respectively.

Thugs' work no longer existed and those who remained serving as employees on the property were called cowboys. It was a year since Dionysus fled the persecution of the men who followed him and six long months when Luz did not see his great love.

The search for the fugitive and his band of criminals continued, however, without any positive effect. Until one day the platoon commanded by Justino and Florêncio received the information that the bandits were in a city to the east of the point where the military camped and planned to carry out a large loot on the local merchants.

Who gave the clue was one of those who previously belonged to the group and who was dismissed, indignant decided to denounce the plans of the old comrades in exchange for not being sentenced to death. The tip was more than useful and as the main target of the searches was the farmer, they agreed to release the informant. That winter afternoon, when the floodgates of the skies seemed to have been opened on purpose and a torrential rain did not stop falling.

Criminals began to invade the establishments, dominating everyone who was there and stealing their belongings. While part of the gang looted businesses the other invaded the homes and stole money, jewelry and even clothes, shoes and food from the residents.

They were aware that the military troops were distant and alien to the trawlers they practiced in that place, but what they did not expect was that one of the rebels would have revealed to their pursuers the place and the exact time when they would commit such a crime.

When they intended to flee from there, taking many animals with heavy loads of the fruit of their thefts, they realized the siege that was made to arrest them, the order of the leader of the pack was one: to die fighting and never surrender.

The exchange of gunfire began, a song made by the buzzing of bullets bouncing off the walls of houses or other targets that were positioned between the two groups of snipers, was heard, while people hid where they could be protected from possible stray bullets, death paraded through the narrow streets of the small town.

The ammunition was running low and a large part of the pack fell to the ground, punctured by bullets from the powerful rifles used by the military. When he realized that his men would not be able to stop his enemies, the leader of the bandits repeated the same feat of years ago and rode on horseback, abandoning to his own luck those who were giving their lives to save him from death. But not every day luck is with someone, there are times when she leaves the man to fend for himself. Especially if he is insensitive and cowardly. Florencio and Jerônimo, always acting in agreement, started to pursue the traitor of their cronies on the road outside.

They surrounded him on the right and on the left, reaching the deserter a few kilometers away. Matching their animals to his, they threw the damn on the ground and dominated him. Then they led the prisoner to the farm where Luz and the others who were terrified by him of the practice of their injustices were found.

After seeing his mother and sister, who, even though they were victims of his wickedness, still mourned his shameful defeat, they took him to the province together with his companions who survived the armed struggle. The Baron of Café finally fell out of favor, was tried and sentenced to death by hanging in a public square.

At the request of the emperor, Countess Lucinete e Florêncio, now with the new title of Baron, and Count Justino were present at the occasion to attend the execution of the condemned and to serve as witnesses of the fulfillment of justice.

Dionysus, who, having lived for several months as an outlaw, among the worst types of individuals, had a full beard. His robes were ragged and filthy, his hair long and waxed by such a large amount of dirt, he didn't seem to be showering for several weeks.

One by one they were hanged, first his crime cronies, then himself. Before being executed, however, standing on the wooden platform made for that occasion, while the executioner put the rope around his neck, he looked at Luz. She was right in front of him like everyone else. who watched the execution in silence. He suddenly looks at her and smiles broadly, seeming to disdain her color. Even in the worst moment of his life, when death was certain.

And his descent into hell was likely that unfortunate still dared to belittle the one who for a long time enslaved. The executioner opens the pit located just below the damned man's feet, leaving him hanging by the neck, kicking while life abandoned him completely.

After the punishment of the culprits is over, all of them leave and the three friends return to their homes, but not before agreeing to meet again at the farm the following weekend. Moment when the Countess's wedding and the new Baron of Café would take place. The ceremony took place on Sunday and dozens of guests were present, including many provincial personalities and the emperor with his entourage of distinguished people.

The small chapel located in the center of the property was duly decorated and there the priest heard the yes of the bride and groom, when they exchanged rings and swore eternal love. After a big party, many animals were killed to feed the huge crowd that had fun all day and night.

The next morning, after everyone was gone, the couple was finally able to have their moment alone and surrendered themselves as the one they truly love deserves. In the days that followed everything was beautiful and wonderful, happiness moved from one place to another, in the same place where one day only pain and sadness made their home, the most complete happiness reigned.

Death was expelled, wickedness destroyed, darkness consumed by the light of justice and mercy. True love prevailed, henceforth only peace would spring up in each heart. In the life of someone who only learned to cry before, a wide smile sprang up, it was the end of a cycle made up of prejudices and tyranny. From then on, only freedom and the chance to be happy mattered. ANGUISH was finally wiped out completely.

End

CPSIA information can be obtained at www.ICGtesting.com
Printed in the USA
LVIW010035020820
662074LV00033B/434